AMATEU

Skye Fargo heard the tinkle of a rein chain behind him. A rider, following him. Another sound came through the darkness, the faint scrape of low branches being moved aside. There was more than one rider following him.

Fargo let his pinto move on slowly as he picked up the sound of a third rider. A tight smile touched his lips. They were amateurs, their efforts crude. His ears told him their every move. He dropped from the Ovaro, spun as he landed on the ground, and his shot caught the first rider as the man came through the trees.

Fargo spun again before the rider hit the ground. His next shot splintered the second rider's cheek with an explosion of bone and blood. The third rider came charging, firing furiously, but Fargo had already hit the ground rolling and landed against a tree. He fired and heard the third rider curse in pain, then race desperately away.

The Trailsman rose and holstered his gun. Amateur night was over. The next time he'd have to take on the best. . . .

NORTH COUNTRY GUNS

THE

TRAILSMAN

159

NORTH
COUNTRY
GUNS

by

Jon Sharpe

Ⓞ

A SIGNET BOOK

SIGNET
Published by the Penguin Group
Penguin Books USA Inc., 375 Hudson Street,
New York, New York 10014, U.S.A.
Penguin Books Ltd, 27 Wrights Lane,
London W8 5TZ, England
Penguin Books Australia Ltd, Ringwood,
Victoria, Australia
Penguin Books Canada Ltd, 10 Alcorn Avenue,
Toronto, Ontario, Canada M4V 3B2
Penguin Books (N.Z.) Ltd, 182–190 Wairau Road,
Auckland 10, New Zealand

Penguin Books Ltd, Registered Offices:
Harmondsworth, Middlesex, England

First published by Signet, an imprint of Dutton Signet,
a division of Penguin Books USA Inc.

First Printing, March, 1995
10 9 8 7 6 5 4 3 2

The first chapter of this book previously appeared in *Texas Terror*,
the one hundred fifty-eighth volume in this series.

Ⓟ REGISTERED TRADEMARK—MARCA REGISTRADA

Printed in Canada

The Trailsman

Beginnings . . . they bend the tree and they mark the man. Skye Fargo was born when he was eighteen. Terror was his midwife, vengeance his first cry. Killing spawned Skye Fargo, ruthless, cold-blooded murder. Out of the acrid smoke of gunpowder still hanging in the air, he rose, cried out a promise never forgotten.

The Trailsman they began to call him all across the West: searcher, scout, hunter, the man who could see where others only looked, his skills for hire but not his soul, the man who lived each day to the fullest, yet trailed each tomorrow. Skye Fargo, the Trailsman, and the seeker who could take the wildness of a land and the wanting of a woman and make them his own.

1861, east of White Bear and west
of Moose Jaw, the province of Saskatchewan
in the wild, untamed land called Canada,
where the only law was lawlessness . . .

1

It was nearing the end of the day when the big man with the lake blue eyes heard the screams while he rode through the forest of balsam fir and white spruce. Skye Fargo reined the magnificent Ovaro to a halt as the screams came again, women's voices, first, then children's, and finally the coarse cries of men. He turned the horse down the slope to his left, skirting the closely packed tree trunks, and when he reached the bottom of the slope he emerged from the forest to see the river in front of him. Two wagons, nondescript, makeshift rigs with canvas tops, were on the other side, and most of their occupants were already strewn across the ground. Yet a furious battle still raged. More than a half-dozen fiercely whooping Indians attacked a lone figure against one of the wagons, a man wearing some sort of uniform with a brilliant scarlet jacket and a Sam Browne belt, black jodhpurs, and a wide-brimmed hat with a high peak pinched in at the top.

He was putting up a fierce fight with a pistol and rifle and two more of his attackers lay on the ground, Fargo saw, but he had dropped to one knee with three arrows in him, two in one leg and a third in his shoulder. But there were just too many for the lone figure. Fargo saw one of the Indians send another arrow into the man as the others rushed to close in. "Damn," he spit out as, out of the corner of one eye, he saw two more Indians still smashing their tomahawks into the bodies strewn across the riverbank. Fording the river in the face of the attack would make him a near-helpless target in midstream, he realized, and he sent the Ovaro racing twenty yards down the bank before turning the horse into the water. The river proved deep, and the pinto had to swim most of the way. When he emerged on the other bank, he saw the scarlet-jacketed figure lying prone on the ground yet still fighting off the blows of his attackers. Fargo drew the big Colt from its holster as he raced the horse toward the wagons, his first object to stop the attackers from killing their victim, and he fired off three shots at a full gallop.

Two of the Indians went down and four others turned to see him charging at them. They scooped up bows and Fargo flattened himself in the saddle as a flurry of arrows sailed toward him. Two rifle shots followed the arrows, and with one quick motion Fargo spun the Ovaro in a tight circle and dove from the saddle on the side away from the Indians. Only a narrow strip of open ground lay between the riverbank and the line of trees, and he hit the ground already rolling. He continued to roll toward the trees as he fired off another shot, and he felt two arrows thud into the soft earth near him. He twisted as he rolled, half dived, and an arrow grazed his leg, but he reached the line of trees and flung himself into the brush. He rolled again, half rose, and dived into a dense thicket of tall fireweed, where he lay motionless on his stomach.

He could peer through the tall brush to see the four Indians move into the trees to search for him. They moved slowly, shadowy shapes in the dimness of the forest and the gathering dusk. They had their short bows drawn, arrows in place on bowstrings, ready to hurl through the air. Fargo's finger rested against the trigger of the big Colt. Once he fired they'd know where he was, he muttered in grim silence. He had to make his first shots count. Hardly daring to breathe, he watched the four searchers move closer, and he waited another dozen precious seconds. One of the Indians moved half behind the figure in front of him. It was the best moment he'd find, Fargo decided, and he raised the Colt as he tensed every muscle of his body. When he pressed the trigger, the two shots sounded almost as one and the first Indian crumpled instantly, the man half behind him doubling in two as the second shot tore through his abdomen.

But Fargo was already flinging himself sideways as the other two Indians loosed their arrows, and he felt one shaft graze his leg as the arrows slammed into the thicket where he'd been. They heard him rolling through the brush and followed with another volley of arrows. Fargo fired a shot as he rolled, not taking enough time to aim. He missed, and both pursuers were almost upon him. He pushed to one knee and had to drop flat to avoid an arrow fired at point-blank range. He glanced up to glimpse the tomahawk coming at him and tried to twist away, but the side of the tomahawk slammed into his right forearm. He felt the revolver drop from his hand as his fingers went numb, and he fell on his back to see the figure diving at him. He managed to get one knee up and let it hit into the man's belly. He heard the Indian's gasp of pain, but the attacker still landed atop him. The man's hands reached to circle his throat, but Fargo felt the numbness fade from his own hand, and he brought his fist around in a short blow that smashed into the side of his attacker's face.

Though awkwardly thrown, the blow was hard enough to knock the Indian half off him, and Fargo was about to push to his feet when he saw the fourth Indian with his bow drawn, waiting for a chance to fire his arrow. Fargo flung himself across the Indian beside him, pulling the man with him as he rolled. The Indian tried to twist away, but Fargo clung to him as a wet leaf clings to a rock, rolling again with his arms wrapped around his foe. The Indian with the drawn bow followed, still trying to get a clear shot. The red man in Fargo's grip cursed, managed to get one arm free, and he brought his hand up, fingers outstretched to jab into his eyes. Fargo turned his head in time to take the stiff-fingered jabbing blow against his temple. Using his superior strength, yet keeping hold of the smaller Indian, he pushed himself upward, taking the man with him. On his feet, head pushing into the Indian's chest and arms wrapped around him, Fargo swung himself in a half circle, exposing himself to the waiting archer. Out of the corner of his eye, he saw the man take a split second to pull his bowstring back a fraction further, and then the arrow flew through the air. Fargo waited his own split second before whirling again with the man in his grasp, and he felt the man's body stiffen as the arrow hurtled into the small of his back.

Unwrapping his arms from the man, he charged forward, knocking aside the falling figure with the arrow almost entirely through his body, to bowl into the other Indian who tried to fix another arrow onto his bowstring. The Indian went down sideways, the arrow falling aside, but he clung to the bow. He hit the ground on one knee, and as Fargo came after him he rose and, using the end of the bow as a spear, thrust it forward with a lunge. Fargo managed to pull his head back as he half twisted, and the bow end all but brushed his face. He sunk a powerful, hooking blow into the Indian's side and felt the snap of one rib as the man cried out in pain. A left cross followed that landed on the man's jaw and the Indian went down and half rolled, but not fast enough to avoid both Fargo's knees as they landed atop his spine. He let out a garbled cry of anguish as his vertebrae snapped, and as Fargo pushed to his feet the man's body twitched convulsively and his hands clasped and unclasped and finally he lay still.

Fargo spun, spied the Colt in the grass, and scooped it up, dropping to one knee, listening. There had been two more Indians by the bodies of the slain travelers, but he heard only silence now. They had fled. He grunted as he rose to his feet and hurried from the trees to the narrow strip of land along the riverbank. He ran to where the scarlet-jacketed figure lay alongside one of the wagons. He dropped down beside the man and saw he was somehow still alive, though bleeding from a dozen wounds. "No, don't try to talk," Fargo said as the man attempted to gasp out a word. Fargo whistled and the Ovaro trotted over. Fargo rose and dug into his saddlebag to find a roll of cloth bandage strips.

He had just dropped down to the barely alive figure when he heard the sound in the trees. He rose instantly, and positioned himself at the edge of the wagon, his eyes on the tree line, when a voice called out, a woman's voice. "Don't shoot," it said and Fargo watched as a short-legged horse and rider emerged from the junipers. He stepped from behind the wagon but kept the Colt in his hand as he watched the horse draw nearer and come to a halt. A young woman, bare-armed in a leather vest and a fringed deerskin skirt that encircled a slender shape, swung from the horse and rushed to the uniformed figure. "Good God, he's still alive," she said.

"Just about," Fargo said.

She leaned over the man. "Thomas, can you hear me?" she asked, and the man managed to move his head. "Hold on. Just you hold on," she said. "We'll get you to a doctor." She lifted her face to Fargo. "I'll help you with the bandages. Sit him up so we can get his jacket off," she said. She rose and went to the pack on her horse as Fargo holstered the Colt, returning with a leather-covered bottle. "Whiskey," she said, and after they had the man sitting up and his jacket off she managed to get some of the liquid down his throat. Fargo's eyes went over the man's body.

"We can only bandage the worst of his wounds," he said grimly, and she nodded and began to use a cloth to wipe some of the blood from the man's body. She worked quickly and deftly beside Fargo as he bandaged the deepest wounds, and he had a chance to look at her again. There was Indian blood in her, he decided. It was in the high-cheekboned contours of her face, in the hint of olive in her skin, and in the slight flare of her nostrils and the thin black eyebrows. It was also in the cool, unflustered gaze she gave him, a kind of pride that bore its own regal stamp. But her eyes were hazel and her long hair, held by a pin at her back, had a tinge of red in it.

"Talk to me while we work," Fargo said. "Who is he?"

"Officer Thomas Moran of the Northwest Mounted Police," she said.

"Who are they? Never heard of them," Fargo said with a frown.

"I imagine you will in time," she said.

"You were with him?" Fargo questioned.

"Yes," she said.

"Who are you?" Fargo asked.

"Lisette Dumas," she answered. "I was hired as a guide for Officer Moran. I know this country very well."

He hesitated a moment as he tightened a bandage and then decided to go on. "What tribe?" he slid at her, his glance quick, and he saw her hazel eyes turn on him, a moment of cool appraisal, and then a half smile touched her lips.

"You're very quick. My hair and eyes fool most people," she said.

"I get paid to see what most people don't see," Fargo told her.

She held the half smile as she continued to study his strong, chiseled face. "My mother was Sekani, my father was a French trapper. I used to help him work his trap lines. When he died, I got work as a guide," she said. "You're not Canadian," she added, the half smile staying.

"That's right. American," Fargo said. "You're quick enough, too." She let the smile widen as she finished tightening the last bandage, and Fargo helped her lay Thomas Moran on his side. The man was still breathing, but he was unconscious, perhaps a merciful state, Fargo reflected, considering his wounds. Lisette Dumas rose, and Fargo pushed to his feet with her. She was taller than he'd first observed, her legs long, smooth, and lovely, ending in narrow hips, the vest covering what seemed to be modest breasts. "Were you with the wagons?" he asked.

"No. We came onto the attack soon after it had started. We saw it from the ridge and Thomas raced down. He told me to stay in the trees. I couldn't have helped him much. I had no gun. He thought they'd run when they saw him."

"He was wrong," Fargo said as he started to make his way through the slain bodies that littered the ground. His lips drew back in disgust at the sight. Every man, every woman, and every child had been shot with arrows or bullets, stabbed with knives, and hacked with tomahawks. He paused beside two of the slain Indians and frowned down at them. "This is one of the most savage attacks I've ever seen," he said.

"Yes, even for the Cree," Lisette said.

"Is that what they are?"

"Western Cree," she said and pointed to a gunshot pouch one of the dead attackers had at his waist. "All that beadwork in flower patterns is always western Cree."

"I'll remember that," Fargo said. "One thing is plain."

"What's that?"

"They didn't want anyone left alive to talk," he said.

"Guess not. But I saw six canoes of Cree in the distance, paddling like all hell downriver," Lisette said, a tiny furrow crossing her smooth forehead.

"You think they were trying to get away, too?" Fargo questioned.

"I don't know, but it sure looked like it," Lisette said.

"You saying this was done by some pack of outlaw Cree? Renegades that everybody's afraid of?" Fargo frowned.

"I'm just telling you what I saw. I don't know what it means," she said.

Fargo grunted and cast a glance across the river. He estimated there was not more than a half hour of day left. "We haven't time to bury all these people. I'll try to find some identification on them," he said, and Lisette nodded and walked back to the unconscious figure of Thomas Moran. She was a strange admixture, he decided. In her hazel eyes he had seen the horror and pain, but her face remained composed and controlled, as though showing emotion were weakness. Perhaps a result of the Indian half of her, he mused. He turned to his grim task and began to go through the clothing of the victims, his lips drawn back in disgust and pity, and finally he stared down at the identification he'd found in pockets and purses.

They were Americans, he found in surprise, migrating to Canada for reasons that had died with them. An unfinished letter in one woman's bag told of their excitement at becoming settlers in a new land. But that had all ended in a brief moment of vicious savagery and, shoving the pieces of identification into his pocket, he walked back to where the young woman knelt beside Thomas Moran as darkness fell.

"We've got to get him to Moose Jaw. There's a doctor there," she said.

"Moose Jaw?" Fargo exploded. "Hell, he'll never be able to ride a mile, much less to Moose Jaw. Isn't there a doctor anywhere closer?"

"No," Lisette said. "Besides, Colonel French is in Moose Jaw, too."

"Who's that?" Fargo inquired.

"His commander," Lisette said.

17

Fargo looked at the silent figure. The man was barely breathing. "The ride will kill him. He'll never make it," Fargo said.

"He might make it by canoe," Lisette said.

"He just might, but we don't have a canoe, honey," Fargo snapped.

"I know where we might get one," she said.

"Where?" Fargo frowned.

"There's a Cree camp about five miles downriver. Maybe we could steal a canoe," she said.

Fargo stared at her. "You're serious, aren't you?" he said.

He chin lifted, and she held almost a chiding challenge in her handsome face, the hazel eyes steady. "It's not impossible," she said.

"Only damn near so," Fargo snapped.

Lisette rested one hand on Thomas Moran's still figure. "I'd like to save his life. He's a good man. Couldn't we try?" she asked.

Fargo swore silently as he turned her plea over in his mind. "No, *we* couldn't try. If there's any chance it'd take one person, no chance of noise, a mistake, one person sneaking into the camp alone. That's the only way it could possibly work," he said.

She glanced at him, the challenging appraisal still in the hazel eyes. "You could do it," she said. "I know you could."

"You know?" he echoed questioningly.

"Yes, something about you. I'd even bet you've done it before," she said.

He grunted and studied her as a half-moon came up. "Maybe, but that doesn't make it any less dangerous," he said.

The challenge left her eyes and her face softened as she lowered herself to the ground, folding long legs under her. "I know. It's asking a lot, more than I've a right to ask. It's just that I was taught never to turn your back on a deserving life, and Thomas Moran is a deserving life."

Fargo lowered himself to the ground beside her as he swore under his breath. She had a simple directness that was all the more powerful because of her sincerity. He swore silently again as he spoke without looking at her. "I'll have to wait till they're asleep. That could be hours," he said and felt her hand come to rest over his, a light, warm touch.

"Thank you," she said. "I'm very grateful to you."

"What the hell," he muttered. "Everyone's allowed a few damn fool things."

She was quiet for a moment and then her voice was soft, a sweet chiding in it. "I think it's time you told me your name," she said, and he suddenly realized the truth in her words.

"Fargo . . . Skye Fargo," he said.

"A good name . . . a very American name. I like it," she said, and somehow made it sound not unlike a regal compliment.

His eyes glanced at the still-breathing figure of Thomas Moran. "You want to tell me about him and what he was all about?" he asked.

"I'd rather Colonel French did that," she said.

"Did Moran hire you to work with him as a guide?" Fargo questioned.

"No, Colonel French did," she said.

"How long did you work with Moran?"

"Three months," she said, and he caught the sharpness

of her sidelong glance. "You're wondering if I was more than a guide," she said.

Fargo half shrugged. "The thought crossed my mind," he said.

"You can uncross it. Thomas Moran was a real gentleman. He respected me. I respected him," Lisette Dumas said. "Maybe that's another reason I want to save him."

Fargo settled back against the wheel of a wagon. "I'm going to get a nap. It's going to be a long night," he said and half closed his eyes and heard Lisette relax beside him. But even dozing refused to cooperate as the parade of thoughts marched through his mind, and he found himself staring up at the half-moon as it slowly wandered across the blue-black velvet sky. He guessed an hour had gone by when Lisette's voice broke into his thoughts.

"You're not napping. You haven't napped at all. What are you thinking about?" she asked softly.

"Everything that's happened here. It wasn't an ordinary attack on a couple of wagons. Hell, I've seen enough of those. They can be vicious but this was more than vicious. Then there were the canoes you saw raving away. There's something more here. I don't know what, but something more," he said.

"Maybe you're right, but we can talk about that later. Right now I just want to get Thomas Moran to a doctor," she said.

Fargo glanced at the moon. Enough time had gone by. It'd take at least another hour to reach the Cree camp. He rose to his feet, reached down, and pulled her up. "Come on," he grunted.

"I thought you said only one person alone had a chance," she said with a frown.

"Get your horse," he said, and she continued to frown as she returned with the short-legged brown gelding and swung into the saddle. Her eyes still questioned as he climbed onto the Ovaro and rode off with her. "I don't fancy walking five miles to the Cree camp, and I don't fancy leaving my horse behind there," he said, and she let the frown slide from her face. He set a nice, steady canter and saw the clouds move across the moon with fitful regularity, and he was grateful for that. He needed only a fitful light and no more.

Lisette rode in silence beside him, and he finally slowed the pace to a walk and finally drew to a halt. He took in deep drafts of the night air and picked up the smell of wood-fire embers and charred trout. "This is as far as you go," he said as he swung from the horse. "Take the Ovaro back with you and wait."

"What if you don't come back?" she asked.

"You'll have a damn fine horse to ride to Moose Jaw," he told her.

"Maybe you shouldn't try it," she murmured.

"Cold feet?"

"Something like that. I'm suddenly afraid for you and maybe ashamed at having asked you to do it," she said.

"Too late, honey. We're here now. Besides, I'd like to keep Moran alive. He may have seen something you didn't from the trees. She took the Ovaro's reins and leaning from the saddle, placed her other hand against his cheek.

"Come back," she murmured as she drew her hand away.

"I aim to," he said and waited till she rode from sight with the two horses. He turned and, falling into a long lope of a stride, made for the Cree camp. He reached it

21

through a line of black spruce and dropped to one knee to survey the camp. It stretched out along the riverbank and Fargo took note of at least a dozen figures asleep on the open ground. There were certainly more in the six teepees he saw. Their teepees were not unlike the conical shape of the plains teepees, but they used many more poles, as many as twenty or more, he counted, and birch-bark rather than hide outer covering.

His eyes moved with the water's edge, and he saw canoes, all pulled out of the water and resting on the river-bank as was the practice of every Indian tribe. Fargo began to edge his way around the top of the camp to the bank where, silent as a water moccasin, he slid himself into the warm river. He let the gentle current push him a few dozen yards to the first of the row of canoes, where he pulled himself from the water to lie on his stomach, his eyes scanning the camp again. There were at least four sleeping figures all too close to the canoes, but there was nothing he could do about that. But his hand crept down to his ankle where the double-edged thin throwing knife rested in its ankle holster. If anything went wrong he'd have only a split second to react with swiftness and silence. There'd be no time to pull his trouser leg up and draw the knife from its holster. There'd be only time to take instant aim and throw. His hand removed the thin blade from the holster and put it between his teeth as he began to crawl forward again.

He half rose at the first canoe and peered inside to be certain it held at least one paddle. He saw two and low-ered himself again. Stretched out almost prone on the ground, he extended his arms to close both hands around the prow. He grasped the top edges of the canoe. Work-ing with absolute caution, he began to slide the canoe toward the water, grateful for the softness of the riverbank soil. Pausing after every few inches to glance up and survey the camp, he continued to slide the canoe forward. It was less than a half-dozen yards to the water, yet it seemed as though it were a mile. There was no weight to the canoe, yet his shoulder muscles cried out from the tensed strain of inching the vessel along silently. He was nearing the edge of the bank, about to congratulate himself on his success, when it happened. The first thing he felt was the slight shiver of the canoe under his hands, and then he heard the sound of the pebble as, dislodged, it began to roll toward the water.

It was a slight, insignificant noise, yet in the silent night it sounded to him as though it were a boulder crashing down a slope. Fargo halted in position and dropped his hands from the prow of the canoe as the pebble rolled into the water with a tiny plink that again sounded disproportionately massive. He raised his head to peer out into the camp and cursed silently as he saw the figure push itself to a sitting position not more than a few dozen yards from him. The Cree sat up and peered through the night toward him. Shit, Fargo muttered silently.

2

The Cree blinked sleep from his eyes as he peered through the darkness, his head cocked to one side, listening. He would focus in on him in a moment, Fargo realized as he pulled the throwing knife from between his lips and, with a single, quick motion, sent it hurtling through the darkness. The Indian never had a chance to see it coming until it imbedded itself in the base of his throat, stopping only where the hilt prevented it from going any deeper. He crumpled backward, a slow motion as if he were returning to sleep. Fargo stayed motionless, not daring to breathe as his eyes swept the other sleeping figures with a quick glance. None moved and Fargo took the prow of the canoe again and silently eased it into the water, pausing every few moments for another quick glance at the camp.

Finally, the stern of the canoe still resting on the shore, Fargo moved back onto the riverbank. The throwing knife had been too valuable for too many years to just abandon it. Besides, it was the only silent weapon he had and might well be needed again. Moving in a crouch, he crept into the camp, reached the slain Cree, and retrieved the blade. He wiped it clean on the grass, returned it to its calf holster, and advanced to the canoe, where he pushed the stern into the water and stepped into the boat. He had begun to let the canoe drift silently from the shore when he heard the sound and spun around to see another of the Cree had come awake. Half standing, the Indian peered through the night at the riverbank and suddenly let out a gutural shout. Fargo saw the other figures quickly coming awake and starting to rise to their feet. He grabbed one of the paddles from the bottom of the canoe and started to send the canoe into midriver. He splashed furiously. There was no more need for stealth as the camp had become awake, and he saw other figures running from the teepees.

Fargo sent the canoe downriver, away from where Lisette waited, and the fitful moonlight let him see the Cree racing for their ponies after a moment of surprised confusion. He was in the middle of the river, paddling hard, when the horsemen raced along the shoreline after him. When they came abreast of him they fired a flurry of arrows that were all wide of their mark. They fired a second flurry which came closer, and Fargo dropped to the bottom of the canoe and drew his Colt. The moon vanished behind a cloud for a moment, and when it reappeared he saw the Cree still riding the shoreline across from him. He fired three quick shots, and two of the Cree went down. The others began to draw back from the water's edge, but Fargo's next shot sent another falling from his pony. The Cree sent their horses back from the shore's edge, but Fargo took aim, fired again, and another pursuer flew from his horse, and this time he saw the Cree pull to a halt.

The moon disappeared again for another long moment, and when it reappeared Fargo saw the Cree had stayed halted. Paddling with one hand, his Colt in the other, he moved the canoe downriver. The Cree stayed in place on the shore. They had plainly decided they'd only lose more braves to continue the pursuit; the price was too high, and he saw them collect the dead and wounded and ride away. He holstered the Colt and continued paddling until he had gone another half mile when he maneuvered the canoe to rest along the shoreline. He used his wild-creature hearing to tell him whether the Cree had decided to come after him again. But only the sound of night crickets came to his ears, and he stretched out in the boat and waited. He let at least another hour go by, perhaps more, before he moved the canoe to midriver, this time paddling upriver. He stopped paddling when he neared the Cree camp, slid over the edge of the canoe into the water, and guided the boat to the opposite bank of the river. He pulled it from the water, hoisted its lightness onto his back, and made his way through the trees in from the river. He slowed when he drew opposite the Cree camp across the river and saw they had two sentries posted, perhaps more behind the teepees.

He continued on, stepping silently in the thick spruce as he cast an eye across the river. Had the band that attacked the wagons come from this camp, he wondered as he moved carefully. He stayed in the cover of spruce until he was beyond sight of the camp before lowering the canoe into the water again. He paddled softly, now, sliding the canoe through the night river until he finally saw the dark shapes of the two wagons on the bank. He paddled to the bank where Lisette was already waiting under a half-moon that had decided to stay out now. "I was growing very worried," she said as he slid the boat onto the softness of the riverbank.

"A few little problems," he said, and his eyes went to the prone figure beside the wagon. "He still alive?" he asked, and Lisette nodded. "Let's get him," he said, stepping onto the shore. She helped him carry the stained and scarlet-jacketed figure to the canoe, where he lay the man gently inside. "You'll take your horse, my horse, and his," Fargo told her. "You just ride along opposite me. I don't think they'll be coming from the camp, but if they do, you take off into the trees." Lisette nodded gravely. "Anybody else we run into will only see me paddling a canoe upriver, and a girl with three horses. How long to you think it'll take us to reach Moose Jaw?"

"You will have to rest some. Even the Cree cannot paddle all night and all day," Lisette said. "By sundown tomorrow, I hope."

Fargo shook his head unhappily, cast an eye on Thomas Moran, and climbed into the canoe. "Start riding," he said. He pushed from the shore and began to paddle, and the night fell silent again. Lisette rode slowly along the shore, keeping pace with him, and he glanced at Moran every half hour as his misgivings rose. The man's wounds were bleeding through the bandages, he saw, and he swore in frustration. But he held to a steady pace that let him go on for longer than frantic hurrying would allow. But when dawn began to streak the sky, he felt the utter weariness of arm and back muscles and he headed to shore, where a thick stand of sandbar willow grew almost to the water's edge.

Lisette halted, dismounted, and helped him pull the canoe deep into the willows. Then he brought the horses inside with her. Moran had uttered a few groaning sounds, but he remained mostly unconscious. Yet his breathing stayed steady enough, Fargo noted. The sun began to filter its way through the long, narrow leaves, and Fargo took off his shirt before he stretched out on the mossy ground. He saw Lisette's eyes move over his muscled torso as she sank down a few feet away. "You are tired, I'm sure," she said.

"You get the cigar," he murmured as he flexed his sore muscles. "I'll take two hours, and then we'll go on again." Lisette settled herself near and lay back, opening the buttons of her vest as she did. The garment fell open enough for Fargo to glimpse the side of one breast, a long, lovely curve of line. But sleep closed his eyes, and it wasn't until his inner clock woke him two hours later that he opened his eyes again. He rose and Lisette woke at the sound, and he saw her pull the vest closed at once as she sat up. She followed him to the canoe, where he saw that Thomas Moran still breathed. Lisette took a moment to wash with the water from the river, running her hands over face and arms in the morning sun. He did the same as she brought the horses from the trees, and he had the canoe in the river when she returned.

Once again, she kept pace with him as he paddled up-river. In midmorning they came onto a party of trappers on a canvas-covered raft. He waved at the men as he paddled past, Moran below their line of vision at the bottom of the canoe. By noon he slowed, his arms hurting, but he forced himself to go on. It seemed miraculous that Thomas Moran still clung to life, he murmured grimly, and the thought gave him new strength. He felt the wetness of his skin as beads of perspiration came with the afternoon sun and he kept going, as if his fingers were forever welded to the paddle. The river grew narrower as the sun moved toward the horizon, and suddenly his eyes narrowed as the shapes appeared in the distance, six canoes moving toward him.

He drew closer and saw at least four Cree in each canoe as they came toward him single file, one closely following the other. He shot a glance across at Lisette as the single thought leapt in his mind. Were these the six canoes she had seen fleeing the scene of the wagon attack? And again, had they really been fleeing? More immediately crucial, would they recognize his canoe as one of their own, even though it bore no Cree markings? There was no time and no place to hide, and he drew the Colt and placed it on the bottom of the canoe beside his right knee. The six canoes were but moments away now. There was a thin Indian wearing only tattered britches sitting in the prow of the first canoe. The two braves behind him paddled and Fargo saw the Indian's eyes narrow at him as he passed. Fargo held his face expressionless as he moved by and passed the second, then the third canoe. The Cree all peered hard at him but continued on their way, though he swore inwardly as he saw one scanning the canoe as he went by.

But they passed him without incident, and he finally allowed himself a long sigh of relief as they faded behind. The palms of his hands were soaked with perspiration, he realized, and he wiped them dry on his trousers before taking up the paddle again. Edging closer to shore, he saw Lisette glance at him as she caught the question in his eyes. "Probably," she called out. "Six racing away. Six coming back a day after. Too much of a coincidence not to be." He nodded agreement and he sailed on, still wondering what it all meant as the questions remained. Had they been part of the main Cree camp downriver? Why did they flee the massacre? Where had they gone? He pushed away the questions and concentrated on paddling as the day began to stretch to an end, and the sun, low on the horizon, outlined the long stands of juniper, black spruce, and quaking aspen.

"What is this river?" he called to Lisette.

"A tributary of the South Saskatchewan. There are a number of them. They have no real names and most join with the Waskanna or the Lanigan at Regina," she said. "You going to stop and rest again?"

"No," he said with a glance at the prone figure in the canoe. "He's on borrowed time now." She nodded and kept pace with him as his paddling grew slower with each passing hour. The day began to darken when the dusk was pierced by the twinkle of lights, and he saw the dark shapes of buildings come into view a quarter mile ahead.

"Moose Jaw," Lisette said, and Fargo found a last burst of strength as he drove the canoe forward. The river ran along one edge of the town, and he saw the line of wood-frame buildings that stretched northward from the shore. He beached the prow of the canoe on the bank as Lisette halted in front of him. "I know where the doctor is. I've been to him enough with my father. I'll fetch him."

"Tell him to bring a stretcher," Fargo said as she left the Ovaro and Moran's horse and rode off at a gallop. Fargo groaned as he slowly stretched arm, shoulder, and back muscles until he brought some measure of elasticity back to them. It was but minutes when Lisette returned, a man wearing a black frock coat and carrying a stretcher hurrying beside her.

"This is Doc Montaigne," she said as the man stepped into the canoe and peered closely at Thomas Moran.

"He's barely breathing," the doctor said. "Get him into the stretcher at once." He rose and helped Fargo lift the prone form onto the canvas stretcher. "My office isn't far," he said as Fargo took one end of the stretcher, and they carried the unconscious man up the slight incline from the shore. The streets of Moose Jaw were crowded and busy, even at the end of the day, and Fargo noted at least two gambling saloons and plenty of one-horse haulage wagons, along with heavier seedbed rigs and not a few timber wagons with reach poles separating the front and rear gears. There were plenty of people on foot but no one cast more than an idly curious glance at the stretcher, Fargo noted.

The doctor's office was a large wood-frame building and Fargo helped lay Thomas Moran on a white-sheeted hospital-style bed where Dr. Montaigne immediately began to examine him. A woman in a blue-gray gown appeared from an adjoining room. "I'll need cotton, bandages, surgical clamps, and another sheet," he said to her. He turned to Fargo. "He's lost a terrible lot of blood. It'll be a while before I know if he can be saved."

"We'll come back," Lisette said. "Meanwhile, we'll be visiting Colonel French at the province headquarters." She turned, and Fargo followed her from the doctor's office. "We'll walk. It's not far," she said when they were outside. He took the reins of the Ovaro while she took the other two horses. The streets had grown less filled with people and they passed a white-painted frame building with two carriage lights outside. "The Moose Jaw Inn. It's used mostly by traveling salesman and government people on their way someplace or another," Lisette said. She drew to a halt a few streets further, where Fargo saw a smaller, neat building and behind it, a stable and a corral.

He read the small plaque nailed over the door of the

building as he dropped the Ovaro's reins over a hitching post: GOVERNMENT OF CANADA—NORTHWEST PROVINCES

Lisette knocked and the door was opened in a moment by a tall man, clothed in a Canadian Army uniform. The shirt was unbuttoned at the neck and he held a cup of coffee in his hand. "Lisette Dumas," he said in surprise.

"Colonel French," Lisette said, and Fargo saw the man's eyes go to him.

"Where's Officer Moran?" he asked.

"He's at Doc Montaigne's. There's been trouble, bad trouble," she said.

"Come in, please," the man said, and Fargo followed Lisette into a comfortably furnished room with a desk at one side, a small sofa and table and chairs at the other, a room that plainly doubled as an office and living quarters.

"Skye Fargo, this is Colonel French," Lisette introduced.

"Lieutenant Colonel George French," the man said as he shook hands. He was taller than he'd first seemed, with graying hair, a straight nose, and intensely blue eyes. "Skye Fargo?" he questioned, and Fargo nodded. "The Trailsman?" Fargo's brows lifted and the colonel laughed. "We've a mutual friend," he said. "General Miles Stanford of your Fifth Cavalry. We've worked together."

"I'm sorry we have to meet under these circumstances," Fargo said.

"Maybe you'd both best tell me about these circumstances. Please sit down," the colonel said, and Fargo slid onto the sofa beside Lisette. She began recounting all she had seen. Fargo took over when she halted, and finally handed the colonel the pieces of identification he'd taken from the victims.

"They were Americans. Somebody might come asking," Fargo said.

"You never know. That's why records are important," Colonel French said as he put the pieces of paper into a desk drawer. "God rest their souls." He sat back and his intense blue eyes moved across Lisette and Fargo. "You both say there was something strange about the attack, but you can't pinpoint it. That fits in with Officer Moran's assignment."

"How?" Fargo queried.

"There have been a number of strange attacks and killings, trappers, miners, lone travelers, and an occasional wagon. They seemed purely random, but as we investigated we decided perhaps they were not so random. All were killed by Cree arrows, all in early morning or near dusk, all alongside or near one of the small rivers that run through this region, much as the one you came onto."

"Are you running some kind of special squad, Colonel?" Fargo asked. "I've never seen the uniform Moran wore."

The man allowed a wry smile. "No, you wouldn't have, but I hope everyone will come to know it one day," he said. "You did a brave thing going to my officer's rescue and bringing him back here. You deserve knowing the whole background of all this." He was about to go on when the knock at the door interrupted him, and he rose to answer. Fargo turned with Lisette as Dr. Montaigne stepped into the room.

"I'm sorry," the doctor said. "I couldn't save him.

He'd simply lost too much blood and his wounds were too deep."

"Thank you for trying, Doctor," the colonel said, and the doctor bowed his way from the room. Fargo's eyes went to Lisette, and he saw the sorrow and pain in her hazel eyes. But there was no trembling lip, no tears brimming in her eyes. Only a terrible sadness in her handsome face, and he turned back to the colonel as the man sat down again. "We'll arrange for a proper military funeral for Officer Moran," the colonel said, his voice heavy.

"You want to put off filling me in?" Fargo asked.

"No, it's even more important, now. You could say I'm here as a harbinger of things to come. There are major changes on the horizon for Canada. I imagine you don't know much about Canadian history, right?"

"You're right."

"In 1670, the Hudson Bay Trading Company received a charter to import furs and skins to England. Within a hundred years, the Hudson Bay Company owned or controlled damn near all of Canada except the Maritime Provinces. But soon it is going to cede all its land to the new Canada Confederation. Best estimates have that happening in about five years from now, when John MacDonald will be the first Prime Minister of all of Canada. Now, the new government knows it will have the problem of governing all this land, and one of the men given this responsibility is Colonel Robertson Ross. Colonel Ross believes that a corps of mounted police officers can do this."

"How many in this corps?"

"Present plans call for one hundred and fifty men," Colonel French said.

"One hundred and fifty men to patrol three hundred thousand square miles?" Fargo frowned.

"A hell of a task, I admit. But we hope to make the Northwest Mounted Police a really superior corps of men. Now, the force can't be established until the government takes over the land ceded by the Hudson Bay Company, but I've been sent to get a hard core of mounted police officers in the field. I want to establish a presence even though we're not official yet. It'll help when the Northwest Mounted Police really move out to patrol the new Canada. What's more, there is an influx of adventurers, many from your country, who want to stir up trouble in what they feel will be a climate ripe for it."

"I'm sure of that," Fargo said.

"There's one more thing. There's a group of shady businessmen who want to cause trouble. They want to prove that the Canadian government can't govern this much land. They want to embarrass the new government and force the provinces to be broken up into small territories they can control. They're led by a man name of Ralph Abernoy. I've met Abernoy. He's handsome, quite a ladies' man, very sharp, and has a reputation for shady dealings. All of this is why the loss of Mounted Patrolman Moran is so crippling to me."

"Yes, I'd say you've a kettleful of trouble," Fargo agreed.

"I've a proposition for you, Fargo," the colonel said. "Miles Stanford has told me quite a bit about you. I'd like you to take Moran's place, at least until I can find someone to bring in from headquarters." Fargo felt his eyebrows lift and the colonel leaned forward in his chair. "I need this, Fargo. I need someone with your talents and your courage. Miles Stanford often spoke about you and the things you've done. I'd be proud to have you wear the uniform of the Northwest Mounted Police, if only for a little while. I couldn't do this once the corps is officially established. All our men will have to be Canadian citizens, then, but now I can do whatever I want, and I want you. I've a uniform in the closet large enough to fit you, and I'll double the usual pay for you."

"Slow down, Colonel," Fargo said with a quick glance at Lisette. She sat with her handsome face impassive. "I'm flattered by your kind words and confidence, but I'm here to see an old friend of my father's who wrote he needs my help."

"Who would that be?" Colonel French asked.

"Man named Horace Danner. He's been one of the trappers for the Hudson Bay Company most all his life. He has a daughter helping him, now."

"I know Horace Danner. We keep a list of all the steady trappers who work regular lines. I understand the girl is a stepdaughter," the colonel said.

"Wouldn't know about that. I've never met her, but from Horace's letter she's only been with him for a year or so," Fargo said.

"You make Danner any promises?" the colonel asked.

"Just that I'd come visit. Maybe that's a kind-of promise to help," Fargo said.

French thought in silence for a moment. "Maybe you can kill two birds with one stone," he said, finally. "Be my man and help Horace Danner. I'd guess he wants you to help him break a new trail."

"I'd guess that," Fargo said.

"You can do that and try to find the answers I want at the same time. You won't be finding them instantly.

You'll have the time and the freedom to roam about for both of us. I've got to get another man in uniform out there at once. It's important that the Cree and everyone else see that. Lisette Dumas would help you as she did Officer Moran. She's still on our payroll and you could use her knowledge of this country."

Fargo shot a glance at Lisette and saw that her face remained expressionless. "Give me till morning. I'd like to sleep on it," Fargo said.

"Of course. But one last thing. You have a stake in this now. The people massacred in those wagons were Americans, Fargo. You owe it to them that they have a measure of justice," the colonel said.

Fargo gave him a wry half smile. "You're not above pulling on any strings you can, are you?" he remarked.

"Desperation breeds shamelessness," the colonel said with a shrug.

"I'll stop back come morning," Fargo said as he rose.

"Why don't you put your horses in our stable? You'll find a stableboy there and he'll take care of Moran's mount, too. I'm sure you can use a real good night's rest. Go to the inn. Tell them I'm picking up the bill. I owe you more for everything you tried to do for Officer Moran."

"Much obliged," Fargo said, and Lisette followed him outside to where they took the Ovaro and the other two horses to the stable behind the colonel's quarters. A young, smooth-faced boy took charge of the horses and Lisette took a small bag with her, and Fargo brought a shirt and a small leather-covered bottle from his saddlebag. She walked to the inn with him with no attempt to make conversation. The desk clerk gave them adjoining rooms. Fargo paused at the door of his. He held up the small bottle as he pushed the door open. "Want to do a last good deed for the day?" he asked. "I'd like this salve rubbed into my back and shoulders."

"Consider it done. I'll be with you in a minute," she said and disappeared into her room. He went into his, found a small, neat space with a bed and a dresser, washbasin, and tub of water in one corner. A kerosene lamp gave a soft light as he turned it up and stripped off his shirt and lay face-down on the bed. He felt his muscles throbbing as he heard the soft knock at the door.

"It's open," he said and half turned to see Lisette enter. She had changed the leather vest and skirt for a light blue, floor-length cotton nightgown, loose-fitting enough that it effectively concealed her figure. She sat down at the edge of the bed as he handed her the bottle. "Wintergreen, balm of gilead, arrowroot, and cajeput oil. It never fails," he said. She poured a little of the salve from the bottle and began to massage it into his aching back and shoulder muscles.

"You have a fine body for rubbing," she said.

"You an expert?" he remarked.

"I've seen enough. There is big, there is strong, and there is big, strong, and beautiful," she said. "Does it bother you to be called beautiful?" she asked, a sly laughter in her voice.

"No. Just never thought of myself as that," Fargo said as Lisette's hands moved back and forth across his muscled body. She had a touch that held a strange combination of opposites, strong yet delicate, sensuous yet impersonal. "You're very good. You do a lot of this?" he asked.

"I used to rub my father's back when the years and the work grew too much for him," she said.

Her fingers massaged his shoulders, and he let out a contented sigh as he turned his head enough to see her. She concentrated on her work, red-tinted hair falling loose around her handsome face, which seemed to hold impassiveness as part of it. "Got any reasons I should take the colonel's offer?" he asked.

"A lot of them," she said. "I want to see whatever's happening stopped. No one's going to want a guide to go anywhere with all this going on. And I'd hate to see Canada broken into a lot of little parcels held by greedy men. Lastly, I don't feel safe here anymore. There's always danger in the wild land but this is different."

"Those are all reasons for you. Got any for me?" he pushed at her.

"I'd say it's a good deal for you," she said. He lifted his head, his glance questioning. "You can help your friend and get paid for it," she finished, and he smiled at her brand of matter-of-fact logic.

She sat up straight, finished, and reached over to take a towel from beside the washbasin to dry her fingers. He sat up and watched the way the loose nightgown fleetingly touched the two round breasts as she put the towel back, a hide-and-seek provocativeness in it. She was really very striking, he decided, beauty mixed with strength and all wrapped in a quiet, controlled impassivity. Perhaps it was her own shield, he wondered. If so, it was fashioned of iron as well as velvet, he wagered silently and swung from the bed as she rose to leave.

"Come by in the morning," he said, walking to the door with her. "Not too early. I'm going to make the most of a good bed."

"I am, too. I've never done this before," she said.

"Done what?"

"Slept in an inn or a hotel," she said, her hazel eyes almost grave. "That surprises you," she added, reading his face.

"I guess so, though maybe it shouldn't," he admitted.

"Good night, Fargo," she said, the seriousness still in her eyes.

"Lisette . . ." he called after her. "You ever smile?"

She turned her eyes on him with no change of expression. "Have you seen anything to smile about?" she asked and hurried away. He closed the door and swore at himself as he undressed and stretched out on the bed. He closed his eyes at once, too tired to think about Colonel French's offer or the strangely fascinating young woman with the quiet logic.

3

He lay in bed for an hour after he woke, uncertain whether it had been Lisette or her quiet logic that had shaped his decision, and more bothered that he didn't want to explore that further. He rose, finally, and was dressed when Lisette appeared, clothed in the leather vest and skirt once more and looking quiet lovely. The inn served sausages, biscuits, and good, strong coffee with a definitely chickory flavor, and he breakfasted with her.

"Made your mind up?" she asked between biscuits.

"Always wondered what it'd be like to wear a uniform," he said.

"Thank you," Lisette said, and he frowned at her.

"Don't run off with the bit, honey. It made sense, that's all," he said.

"Whatever you say. You made the decision. You know why," she said, and he frowned at her faintly arched brows and the hint of smugness in her face.

"Let's go see the colonel," he muttered and knew she had to hurry to keep up with his long-legged strides.

"I'll get the horses," she said when they reached the government office, and he entered to find the colonel behind his desk with a young aide.

"That'll be all, Jenkins," the colonel said and fastened his intensely blue eyes on his visitor.

Fargo shrugged. "Why not?" he said, and the delight flooded the colonel's face.

"Good man," Colonel French said and opened a closet door to bring out the scarlet coat on one hanger, the rest of the uniform on another. "You can change in the next room," he said, and Fargo took the uniform from him. He changed quickly, donning the black riding britches and matching high boots, first, then the brilliant scarlet jacket. Everything fitted well, he was glad to find as he strapped on the Sam Browne belt and stepped into the other office.

"Your holster but my gun," he said to the colonel.

"Whatever you're comfortable with, Fargo," Colonel French said. "You know the first thing I want you to chase down, but remember that you represent the Northwest Mounted Police, now. You have the right to make arrests and take action in anything that needs your presence. You'll have my full backing, and remember we've a jail that'll hold up to eight prisoners."

"Good enough," Fargo said. "You'll hear from me when I've something to tell you."

The colonel handed him two folded pieces of paper. "Your official papers, in case the uniform isn't enough for some people. We've been getting recognition, but there are too many who'd like to ignore us. Don't let them."

"I've never liked being ignored," Fargo said.

"Good luck to you," the colonel said, and Fargo strode from the room to where Lisette waited outside with her mount and the Ovaro. He saw the hazel eyes study him for a moment as he put his clothes and holster into his saddlebag.

"Handsome," she said. "Even more than before."

"I guess that calls for a thank you," he remarked.

"It was an observation, nothing personal," she said coolly.

"Good," Fargo said. "I saw a saddle shop when we came in last night. My saddle blanket's getting real worn. I want to get a new one." She nodded and fell into step beside him as he walked down the main street, aware of how many eyes took in the handsome scarlet jacket. He halted when they came to the saddle shop, which, he noted, was diagonally across from the town saloon.

"I'll wait out here," Lisette said, and he stepped into the store where a middle-aged woman in a print dress gave him an approving glance.

"You're another of those new Mounties, aren't you?" she remarked.

"Yes, ma'am," he said as he looked over a stack of saddle blankets in a neat pile.

"God knows we need some law and order nowadays, all kinds of riffraff coming around now that word's out that Hudson Bay's giving up their land and nobody knowing what the government's going to do," she said.

"We'll do our best," Fargo said. He chose a dark red blanket and pulled it from the stack. He was paying for it when he heard the loud voices outside, one a deep, growling voice, and then he heard Lisette snapping out words. The blanket under one arm, he started from the store when he heard Lisette's voice again, higher, now, angrier, and then a sharp gasp of protest and then the growling voice in a bellow of angry pain. He strode from

43

the store to see Lisette pull away from a burly man in a red-checked shirt who held up one hand with a small trickle of blood running across his fingers.

"Little bitch bit me," the man snarled.

"*Bâtard*. Keep your hands off me," Lisette spit out. The man made a lunge for her, but she nimbly twisted away before two men seized her from behind.

"Take her in the back room behind the saloon. I'm goin' to teach the bitch a lesson," the man roared.

"Let her go," Fargo interjected as he lay the blanket across the Ovaro's saddle. The burly figure turned to him, and he saw a broad, coarse face, a flattened nose, and eyes with thick folds under them. He also took in a thick neck and heavily knotted shoulders visible under the red-checked shirt.

"You're one of them new Mounties," the man growled. "Well, sonny, keep your nose out of this."

"Let the girl go," Fargo said.

"You keep hold of the slut," the man threw at his friends without taking his eyes from the red-jacketed figure in front of him. "And you get the hell out of here, sonny. This is the last time I'm goin' to tell you."

Fargo's eyes went to Lisette. "What's this all about?" he asked.

"His name's Zach Croatie. He's a cheating, lying thief," she said.

"I'll shut your damn mouth," the man roared and started toward Lisette again. Fargo saw the crowd gathering but staying back, beyond a long public trough on the other side of the street, and he drew the big Colt as he stepped forward.

"Hold it right there, mister," he said, and Zach Croatie turned to him, fury in his broad face, but his eyes taking in the gun. "Just you simmer down," Fargo said, and his glance went to the two men holding Lisette. "I told you to let her go," he said, his voice taking on a new firmness.

"Go to hell," Zach Croatie said.

"I think some time behind bars might cool you down," Fargo said. He started to move toward the burly figure when the blow struck him from behind, hard enough to send him falling forward. He hit the ground and felt his gun skitter from his hand. Half turning, he saw the man who had sneaked up behind him holding the rifle butt, and Fargo rolled again as he heard the footsteps at his left. Zach Croatie's kick half missed but had enough force to send Fargo sliding sideways across the ground. He let himself roll again and leapt to his feet, the back of his head still throbbing. The burly figure advanced toward him, arms half outstretched.

"I'm gonna smash you in pieces, lawman," Croatie said with a half snarl, half smile twisting his mouth. He followed his threat with a sudden lunge, but Fargo stepped back, rose on the balls of his feet, and danced away from another lunge and then a wild-swinging blow. He stepped in with two quick, hard jabs that landed on the man's jaw and made him blink. But Zach Croatie came forward again, his punches less wild as he tried a short left hook and then a straight right. Fargo parried both blows, but he could feel the power of the man as he moved sideways, and landed another pair of quick jabs. Again, the man blinked but came forward, and Fargo stepped back, planted his feet solidly, and lashed out with a whistling left cross that landed on the point of Croatie's jaw.

His head snapped back and he halted for a moment

and Fargo swore as he failed to follow through at once. The man shook his head and swung again. His thick neck could absorb a lot of punishment, Fargo realized, and he backed away from a series of wild swings, jabbed again, moved from side to side, and saw Zach Croatie's eyes mirror frustration. Suddenly, Croatie lowered his head and charged, bull-like, with a roar of rage. Fargo stepped backward and found himself against the edge of the trough as Croatie charged. He let the man's outstretched arms reach him, Croatie's hands closing to encircle his throat and, using all the strength of his biceps and shoulders, drove a short, straight, underhand right into the pit of the man's stomach. Croatie let out a wheezing gasp of air and dropped to one knee, his hands sliding down from Fargo's throat. Fargo crossed a whipping left hook that turned Croatie's head half around as it sent him sprawling to the ground.

Croatie lay there for a moment, shaking his head in an effort to clear it. Slowly, not unlike a stunned ox, he turned onto his back and sat up on his elbows. Then Fargo caught the movement of his right arm as he reached for his gun. Moving with precision and speed, Fargo let Croatie clear the gun from his holster before he kicked out and sent the weapon sailing into the air. He reached down, big hands curling around Croatie's shirtfront as he lifted the man to his feet and flung him into the water trough. Ducking around to the far side of it as Croatie's head surfaced, he pushed the man under the water again, and his eyes went to the two men holding Lisette and the third one still clutching the rifle.

"Let her go or he doesn't come up again," Fargo said, keeping one hand on Croatie's head beneath the water of the trough. The two men stepped back from Lisette, who swung free at once. "Get my gun," he called to her, and she scooped up the Colt and brought it to him. Taking the pistol from her, he drew his hand out of the trough as he aimed the gun at the trio. "Drop your guns," he said as Croatie's head came up, coughing up water as he tried to draw in air. "I'm only going to tell you once," Fargo said to the trio. The one with the rifle dropped his gun, and the one beside him did the same, but the third one decided to draw. He hadn't his gun out of the holster when Fargo's shot sent him sprawling backward with a cascade of red.

Croatie was still sputtering but getting his breath back as Fargo stepped a pace from the trough. "Climb out of there," he ordered, and the man obeyed, still wheezing as he slipped and fell onto the ground getting out. "Talk," Fargo bit out.

"Been lookin' for her for a year," Croatie gasped between deep breaths as he leaned against the trough. "Bitch stole from me."

"Liar," Lisette cut in, the single word a spear.

"You want to explain?" Fargo asked her.

"Later," she said. "It'd take too long now."

"All right," Fargo said. He spun Zach Croatie around and pushed the barrel of the Colt into his neck. "You're going behind bars. Start walking," he said, and the man obeyed. As he neared the other two, Fargo's eyes went to them. "Fall in ahead of him," he ordered, and the two men glumly obeyed.

"You got nothin' to hold us," Croatie growled.

"Assault on this young woman, drawing your gun on a police officer. That'll do," Fargo said, and the man fell silent. Colonel French was outside with two of his men when they reached the government houses. Fargo saw

47

his eyes widen. "Didn't expect to be back so soon," Fargo said. "Put these three away. I'll fill out the arrest forms."

"Lock them up," the colonel ordered his men.

"You send somebody to bring Jack Bailey down here," Croatie said as he was led away. Fargo stepped into the office with the colonel as Lisette followed. Fargo explained what had happened as he filled out the charge forms.

"Who's Jack Bailey?" he asked when he finished.

"A lowlife but clever lawyer. Croatie's used him before," the colonel said.

"You know Croatie?" Fargo asked with some surprise.

"Yes, he's been here before. He's a schemer and a cheater but he's clever enough to keep eluding serious jail time," Colonel French said. "Bailey will post bond and I'd guess he'll be out in a few days, with Bailey setting down all sorts of explanations and defense motions."

"There was a fourth one you can send the undertaker to pick up," Fargo said. "I'll be on my way again."

"Better luck this time," the colonel said as Fargo left with Lisette at his heels. Outside, he swung onto the Ovaro and held the new saddle blanket on his lap.

"Now you want to tell me what that was all about?" he said to Lisette.

"About a year ago he hired me as a guide. He was freighting meat over a new route. He agreed to pay me half when we started and the rest when we finished. But he didn't come up with the first half. He had excuses, said he had to get to a bank along the way. But there was no town with a bank and when we were halfway through the trip he told me he wouldn't be paying anything till it

48

was over. By then I'd found out he was freighting rotten meat to swindle a buyer somewhere, and I'd had enough. I told him to pay me the first half and he just laughed at me," she said. "I waited and watched and found out he had a bag he guarded all the time. One night I took the bag. As I suspected, it was full of money."

"How'd you get hold of the bag?" Fargo asked.

"I put him into a deep sleep with a rock," Lisette said, "took the money he'd agreed to pay me, and lit out."

"And now he suddenly met up with you," Fargo said. Lisette nodded, and Fargo gave her a long glance. Her quiet, controlled expression hadn't changed, but as he'd guessed, it was a mask for a lot of determination and fire.

"Where now?" Lisette asked.

"Toward White Bear, the place we met, and then on to Horace Danner. His place shouldn't be far from there," Fargo said.

"It's not," Lisette said.

"You know Horace Danner?" Fargo questioned.

"No, but I've passed his place and heard of his operation. He used to be a big supplier for the Hudson Bay people, but I heard he's been having troubles," Lisette said.

"Let's make time," he said and put the pinto into a trot, following the river back all the way until they reached the spot where the wagons stood, silent markers to massacre. "Think we can make Danner's place before dark?" he asked Lisette. She nodded, pointed north across the river, and Fargo moved the Ovaro into the water, his thoughts still lingering on the massacre. "We'll mostly be riding and exploring, but I'd like to find someplace to use as a base," Fargo said as they crossed the river.

"There's a cabin Moran used, about halfway to the Danner place. We can pass it on the way if you like," Lisette said, and he agreed with a nod and followed her as she veered her mount northwest. They had ridden another twenty minutes, he guessed, when they crested a rise. He pulled to a sharp halt. A half-dozen Indians crossed their path and his eyes fastened on their moccasins. "Cree," he muttered. "They've seen us. Get ready to hightail for that stand of spruce." But the horsemen only paused and went on their way as Fargo watched them disappear down a passage between a growth of chokecherry. "They didn't pay us any mind at all," he muttered.

"Maybe your idea about an outlaw band is right," Lisette said. "Or maybe it was because we don't have any wagons with anything to take."

"That's not it. The raid on the wagons was to kill everybody, not to rob," Fargo said.

"Then they were on their way someplace and didn't want to bother with us. We were just lucky," Lisette said and moved her horse forward only to rein to a halt to stare back at Fargo. He sat unmoving, a frown pressed into his brow. "What is it?" she asked.

"Luck," he said. "You hit on it. That's what it was all about, bad luck."

It was Lisette's turn to frown. "I don't understand," she said.

"The people in the wagons, they had the bad luck to be in the wrong place at the wrong time. They saw something they shouldn't have seen. That's why every

50

one of them had to be killed," Fargo said as he spurred the Ovaro forward.

"But what?" Lisette asked.

"If I knew that I'd know everything," Fargo said. "But that's the answer I have to get."

"What about the Cree that seemed to be racing away from the attack?" Lisette said, riding beside him.

"That'll fall into place when I get answers," Fargo said.

"But it could still be an outlaw band," Lisette said.

"It could be," he agreed, and Lisette turned up a small rise. He let his eyes take in natural markers, an automatic habit, as natural as breathing to him. When she turned again, passing two unusually tall white spruce, he saw the cabin appear, a solidly built structure with good saddle-notched logs and a roof of good spruce shingles. He dismounted and stepped inside the cabin, where he saw a thick drape curtained off one half, making two rooms of the interior. A hearth took up one wall and a mattress rested against the opposite wall with the cover covered with Indian blankets. "This'll do fine," he said. "Now let's get to Horace Danner."

He kept the pace at a steady trot, and the day still clung to the land when he reached the Danner place. He took in a modest main house with a smaller house a few dozen yards from it, four drying and storage sheds behind, and a stable at one side. A thousand yards away he saw the blue line of a creek with a half-dozen canoes and rafts drawn up on shore and the cleared land ending in a thick stand of white spruce and paper birch. The door of the main house opened, and Horace Danner strode out, and Fargo found himself staring at the man. It had been a good number of years since he had last seen Horace

Danner, but he hadn't expected a face so visibly older, so worn and tired, hair that had been grayish now white, blue eyes sunken into their sockets, and what had been a lean, lanky frame now drawn in on itself.

"Fargo," Horace Danner called out as he rushed forward. "By God, you're here."

Fargo dismounted, forcing the surprise from his face. "Hello, Horace, old friend," he said. "Sorry I took so long, but I had a job to finish in the Dakota territories. He turned to Lisette as she dismounted. "This is Lisette Dumas. She's helping me learn this land of ours."

"Welcome, girl," Horace said, but his eyes returned to sweep the scarlet jacket and black riding britches. "But what are you doing in that outfit, Fargo? That's the uniform of one of those new Northwest Mounties."

"Bulls-eye, Horace," Fargo said.

"You're one of them?" Horace frowned in disbelief.

"For a little while," Fargo said.

"Then you're not here to help me out?" Horace said.

"Yes, I am. I figure I'll be able to do both," Fargo said. He paused as the door of the second house opened and a young woman stepped out wearing a brown, wraparound skirt and a tan blouse that clung to very full, very round breasts. He took in a compact figure, wide and well-covered hips, and sturdy yet shapely enough legs and a face framed by almost blond hair, a short, stubby nose, and very clear sharp blue eyes and full lips, everything adding up to a feeling of energetic assurance that radiated from her.

"This is my daughter, Caryn," Horace introduced. "Caryn, this is Skye Fargo, who I've been telling you about. Seems he's become a Mountie, but he's still going to help us."

"I heard," Caryn Danner said, and Fargo caught the coolness in her tone as her sharp blue eyes studied his chiseled face. "I'd like to hear more about that," she said with a sniff. Her eyes went to Lisette for a moment with the barest acknowledgment.

"And I want to know why exactly you sent for me, Horace," Fargo said, taking his eyes from Caryn Danner.

"Let's go inside where we can talk," Horace said and led the way to the house, Caryn at his heels, and Fargo let Lisette come alongside him.

"I can wait outside," she murmured.

"Why?" he said, the question more than a question, and she fell silent. The house was well appointed with a long settee, chairs, and braided rugs. Horace Danner sank into one of the chairs and motioned Fargo and Lisette to the settee. Caryn perched herself on the edge of another chair and the wraparound skirt parted enough to show beautifully rounded, firm knees and the beginning of a smooth thigh.

"Hell, Fargo, how'd you get into being a damn Mountie?" Horace Danner asked, slapping his knee.

"Got involved in a Cree attack on two wagons and Colonel French at Moose Jaw convinced me he needed help. Seems the Cree have been causing trouble around here lately," Fargo said.

"They sure aren't acting the way they used to," Horace said.

"Meaning what exactly?" Fargo questioned.

"They were my main suppliers of pelts and hides and now they're not bringing me anything," Danner said.

"Why not?"

"Caleb Barton's got a hand in it."

"Who's Caleb Barton?" Fargo asked.

53

"A damn poacher who's trying to put me out of business," Horace Danner exploded. "I'm sure he's found some way to stop the Cree from selling to me."

"Why'd you send for me, Horace?" Fargo queried.

"With Hudson Bay going to cede its land to the government, everything's changing. The trapping business has gone way down. A collection of newcomers are trying to come into it. I need new lines and new routes. I can't do that and tend to whatever business I have left. That's why I need you. Caryn will back up everything I've said."

Fargo's eyes went to Caryn Danner, and she offered a careful smile. "More or less," she said.

"What's that mean?" Fargo questioned.

"It means Caryn disagrees with me on some things," Horace Danner cut in with obvious annoyance.

"That's true. Horace and I have our differences. But that's not what's bothering me, now. I'm afraid I'm very disappointed in you, Fargo," Caryn said.

"Hell, you haven't had time for that," Fargo said with a frown.

"That uniform is enough. You can't help Horace and work for Colonel French. You can't do both, and Horace told me you were coming here for him. Obviously you haven't," she said firmly.

"What do you want me to do?" Fargo asked.

"Help Horace. Find those new routes for him. That'll be a full-time job. Turn in that uniform. Resign from the Mounties. Concentrate on helping Horace."

"You speak your mind, don't you?" Fargo said, and her sharp blue eyes studied him for a moment, frank appreciation in her gaze.

"So do you, I'd guess," she said.

"That's right, and I still think I can do both," Fargo said. Caryn Danner's expression hardened.

Horace cut in again. "Guess we'll have to live with that, Fargo. Beggars can't be choosers," he said.

"Horace's choice of words, not mine," Caryn snapped.

"Look, if I see it's not working out, I'll turn in the uniform and give all my attention to you folks. After all, I did come here to help Horace," Fargo said. Caryn's face softened a fraction. "I'll start tomorrow," he said as he rose.

"That's fair enough," Horace said warmly, and Lisette rose with Fargo as he started for the door. Horace went with them, but Caryn hung back.

"Fargo," she called, her voice soft, and he turned to her as Lisette went outside with Horace. "There's more here than it seems. Can we talk alone?" she asked.

"I'll try to stop by in a day or so," Fargo said.

"The sooner the better," she said, and suddenly he felt her hand in his, a warm, firm grip. "I know you mean well. You'll pay attention to the things I have to tell you. I'll be waiting for your visit." She pulled her hand away and hurried from the room, well-covered hips and a very round rear swinging beautifully. He went outside to where Lisette was waiting in the saddle.

"Let's get back to the cabin. We can start from there come morning," he said as he swung onto the Ovaro.

"What was that all about?" Lisette asked as she rode off beside him.

"She has some things to tell me," Fargo said.

"Things she plainly didn't want to say in front of Horace. You notice she never called him 'Father'?"

"Maybe because he's her stepfather," Fargo said. "I'll be finding out next time I see her. She was really much more angry about my being a Mountie than Horace was."

"I wondered about that," Lisette said.

"Protectiveness, I'd guess," Fargo offered.

"Maybe."

"Maybe? What's that mean?" he questioned.

"She doesn't seem the protective type to me."

"How do you come to that? You don't know her," he said.

"Some knowing's from outside, some from inside," she said with a quiet certainty that required no comment. He rode in silence until they reached the cabin, and he took care of the horses, unsaddling both and tethering them behind the cabin where a tarpaulin weather cover afforded shelter. When he entered the cabin, he heard Lisette behind the drape that made the cabin into two rooms. He undressed and lay down on the mattress, pulling the sheet over his abdomen as Lisette came from behind the drape. She wore the loose cotton nightgown that enveloped her and lowered herself to the edge of the mattress where a shaft of moonlight gave her a pale loveliness that softened the strength in her face. She leaned forward, wordlessly, and suddenly her lips were on his, a soft pressure with the same strange admixture he'd felt through her fingers, sensual yet somehow impersonal.

"Why?" he said when she pulled back, and the loose nightgown fleetingly touched the twin mounds of her breasts.

"For stopping Zach Croatie," she said. "And for believing the things I told you."

"You always thank people that way?" He smiled.

Her handsome, high-cheekboned face remained unsmiling. "No," she said. "And I don't much like most people, but I like you, Skye Fargo. My mother's people have a saying: A good tree stands firm and gives comfort. I think you are a good tree, Fargo."

"I guess it's my turn to say thanks," he answered and reached up, closing his hands around her shoulders. "I like your way," he said and drew her down to him. He kissed her, and she didn't pull away, her mouth soft yet firm, a response that was not quite a response, and finally he pulled back.

"Good night," she said, rising, still unsmiling, and he watched her disappear behind the drape, lost in the loose nightgown.

4

When morning came, he woke first, washed, and dressed by the small wall at the side of the cabin. Then he fed and saddled the horses as Lisette rose. She was finished when he brought the horses around, beautifully slender in the leather vest and fringed deerskin skirt, and he saw the sun catch the hints of auburn in her hair. "I want to patrol the river for starters, from up in the low hills. Maybe we'll come onto something and maybe we won't. Either way it'll give us an idea of what's going on," he said. "You ride north and I'll go south."

"What if I see something?" she asked.

"You just watch and stay out of sight. We'll meet where the wagons were hit in midafternoon," he said with a touch of severity.

"What if you see something? You just going to watch?" Lisette slid at him.

"Depends," he half shrugged.

"I guess I'll know about that if you don't meet me later," she said. "What do I do then?"

"Report to Colonel French," he said.

Her hazel eyes held his unblinkingly. "One condition," she said.

"Go on."

"You be as careful as you want me to be."

He felt the wry smile come to his lips. "Fair enough," he said, and she rode away without another word. Or a smile. He turned the Ovaro and headed south, staying in the low hills where he had a good view of the river. He drew to a halt only when he came in sight of the Cree camp below. He had seen Cree canoes along the river, some singly, some in pairs. Some hugged the shoreline checking trap lines while others moved silently offshore, trying to spear beavers. He was watching the camp when he saw three canoes arrive from downriver. They halted, and Cree from the canoes went ashore to join the others in the camp.

Fargo's eyes were narrowed in thought as he watched. The Cree sailed southward from the camp as well as north, he pondered, and he slowly moved past the camp below to follow the river further southward. He had gone some three miles, watching the beauty of the land. It was indeed a paradise of riches, for those who wanted only to watch and enjoy and for those who wanted to hunt. He saw marten, blue mink, muskrat, wolverine, and ferret, the ubiquitous beaver, black bear, and grizzly, white-tailed deer, and he spotted signs of wolf and woodland caribou. He'd ridden some three miles south downriver when the hills began to slope to an end and he found himself riding alongside the river. He finally halted, and he was about to turn back when he heard the unmistakable whinny of a mule.

The sound had come from a clump of sandbar willow closer to the river, and he carefully pushed his way into the open. The whinny came again, definitely from inside the willows, and, the Colt in hand, he moved the Ovaro forward through the long, narrow leaves and pulled to a halt as he spotted the mule. He swung to the ground and advanced toward it as he saw that it was a pack mule, double-rigged, with shovels, pans, and pickaxes part of its pack, a prospector's mule. He went a dozen steps further when he saw the man's body on the ground, a gray-bearded elderly man on his back, staring skyward through lifeless eyes. Three arrows protruded from his chest, and his head still oozed clotted blood where his skull had been smashed in. Fargo's eyes grew narrow as he spied the swath of flattened soil beyond the old prospector. The man hadn't been slain in the thicket of willows; he had been dragged into the trees. Fargo followed the trail out of the willows and onto the riverbank, where the patch of drying blood marked the spot of the attack.

He dropped to one knee, his trailsman's eyes surveying every mark and outline in the soil, and he spied the prints of moccasins leading up from the shoreline. The Cree had beached their canoes and come ashore. He grunted and the furrow began to dig into his brow as he picked up more prints. No moccasins, these, but hoofprints, at least four horses, he estimated. But no unshod Indian ponies. The prints were made by horses wearing shoes. The furrow stayed with him as he examined the prints. It was a new turn, one that only added more questions. It seemed others were waiting to meet the Cree when they came ashore. But one thing remained the same. Like those in the wagons, the old prospector had been at the wrong place at the wrong time. He, too, had seen something he wasn't supposed to see.

But what? The question danced, unanswered, as Fargo climbed back onto the Ovaro and began to retrace his way northward. Staying in the low hills once again, he passed the Cree camp as the afternoon sun drifted across the sky. Lisette was there when he reached the meeting place, and her astute, probing hazel eyes pierced into him at once. "Something happened," she said flatly. He nodded and quickly told her what he had come upon. When he finished, she frowned back. "It doesn't fit," she said. "The wagons were attacked by Cree on ponies, you saw that for yourself, and I saw other Cree paddling away as fast as they could."

"I saw that and I didn't look any further," he said. "You stay here." Dismounting, he walked down the slope to where the wagons rested. He drew in his breath as he passed the slain forms, his eyes sweeping the river-bank soil, first, then back toward the treeline. He had almost reached the edge of the trees when he halted. His eyes narrowed as he spotted the line of hoofprints near the spruce, each with the sharp, clear edge of shod hooves. He was still frowning in thought when he returned to Lisette. "I should have looked more carefully. There's a set of shod hoofprints. Two horses, I'd guess, and they went into the trees."

"Then others beside the Cree were here, too," Lisette said.

"Probably," he said.

"Probably?" she echoed. "You just said as much."

"I said what it looks to be. First thing you find out when you learn to track is how easy you can be fooled. Part of reading signs is not just what you see but what it might mean. Does a man have a limp or is he carrying something that makes him seem to limp? Is a horse shortening its stride because it's tiring or because it doesn't like the terrain? Signs alone are not everything."

"Meaning what here?"

"The Cree could be riding their Indian ponies and shod horses they'd stolen. That'd explain the two sets of hoofprints," Fargo told her.

"And leaves us nowhere." Lisette sniffed.

"No. It tells us the Cree could've met others, but we can't be sure yet," Fargo said as he climbed onto the Ovaro. He led the way onto a series of ridges with little tree cover. They had started down over the last one when the six riders came into view and immediately swerved toward them, led by a man wearing a wide-brimmed, black Stetson. Fargo reined to a halt as the man came up to him with his five companions, all ordinary-enough looking range hands, Fargo saw in one quick glance.

"This is luck. I was hoping I'd run into you," the man said, and Fargo took in a heavily lined face, dark-complexioned with a large nose and dark eyes that glittered, a face that wore built-in belligerence. "You're the one that wants to help Horace Danner," he half sneered.

"News travels fast. Who might you be?" Fargo asked.

"Caleb Barton," the man said, and his eyes moved over Fargo's scarlet jacket. "Heard you were one of those new Mounties. Seems you like looking for trouble all over."

"Is that what I'm doing?" Fargo asked mildly.

"If you help Horace Danner you are," Barton said.

"Is that a warning?"

"Call it whatever you want, mister, but you leave Horace Danner to himself. He's like a rotten apple ready to fall. I'm not having anybody pull him up," Barton said.

"Because you want to take over his business."

"That's right. Hudson Bay isn't protecting their people the way they once did. It's every man for himself, now, and he can't cut it anymore. Leave him be."

"I owe the man a favor. Besides, it's a big country. You've room to cut your own way," Fargo said.

"Don't be helpin' Horace Danner. I won't tell you again," Caleb Barton said with a growl.

"I don't take much to threats," Fargo said, and Barton's glance went to Lisette.

"What part's she got in it?" he asked.

"She's helping me," Fargo said.

"I'll bet she is," the man said with a sneer.

"Watch your tongue, Barton," Fargo said.

"Watch your neck," Caleb Barton said, and his men followed him as he rode away.

"He could be all talk," Lisette offered.

"No. There's too much angry ambition in him," Fargo said, moving the Ovaro forward. "There's got to be a town nearer than Moose Jaw around here."

"Yes, Mallardsville, just north. Why?" Lisette said.

"Want a place to nose around, ask questions. Sometimes that turns up things," Fargo said. "But maybe I'll get further without the uniform."

"You might get further with it. People will talk to a lawman where they won't to some stranger passing through. Besides, Colonel French feels it's important to wear it," Lisette said. He smiled inwardly at her loyalty to the colonel.

"Maybe." Fargo shrugged. "You go back to the cabin and I'll be in later tonight." He turned the pinto north and moved through the rapidly falling dusk. The night lay over the land when he rode into Mallardsville. The town turned out to be exactly what he sought, small, rough-edged, populated by trappers, range hands, skin buyers, and equipment salesmen. The saloon was the usual sawdust-floored room with a half-dozen wood tables and a bar along one side. Fargo took in a half-dozen young women with worn smiles as they moved among the already crowded tables. He also took note of how almost all eyes paused to glance at him as he entered in his scarlet uniform and stepped to the door.

"Welcome to Mallardsville, Mountie," the bartender said, a small, wiry man with graying hair and a ruddy face. "This a social or an official visit?"

"Social," Fargo said. "Sort of a fishing expedition, you might say." He paused, aware that more than a few others were listening. "There have been some strange Cree attacks. I'd listen to anyone with anything to tell me," he said.

"Damn strange, that's what it's been," a tall, thin man spoke up. "I passed a dozen Cree the other day and they didn't trouble me one damn bit. But Bill Blaisdel was heading for the river one morning when he was chased for damn near a half mile."

Another man cut in. "Some days they pay you no mind. Others they attack the minute they see you," he said. "Nobody's got any answers, but we're all plenty scared."

"Can't blame you. Let me know anything else funny you come onto," Fargo said.

"Talk is you're helping Horace Danner find a new route," a smaller man mentioned.

"I'm here to help anybody in any way I can," Fargo said, choosing his words carefully.

A rough-faced man spoke up. "You're wasting your time out here, Mountie. No fancy red uniform's going to keep the law in all this territory."

"You might all be surprised one day," Fargo said as the others fell back to muttering amongst themselves. He turned to the bartender. "A barkeep hears more than anybody. I hoped you might have something to toss my way," he said.

"No more than you've heard from the others. But I know somebody you ought to talk to, old Asa Hoddy. Asa's been a part of this country for seventy years. He's seen them all come and go, the trappers, the hunters, the Hudson Bay people, the Cree, the land developers, the new Dominion officials, and the old government holdouts, and he's lived through it all. If anybody knows anything it'd be old Asa Hoddy."

"I'll pay him a visit. Much obliged," Fargo said.

"Go west from town, turn into the hills at Three Rocks," the bartender said. Fargo nodded back and walked from the saloon, aware that not a few eyes followed his departure. Outside, he swung onto the Ovaro and followed the man's instructions and finally made his way into the hills, where he found plenty of black spruce and quaking aspen. He found the small square of yellow light, which turned out to be a sturdy hut with the door ajar. The figure came to the door as he drew to a halt, and Fargo saw a grizzled face above a pair of tattered longjohns.

"Asa Hoddy?" Fargo called. "The barkeep at Mallardsville said I might pay you a visit."

"Come closer, mister," the man said. Fargo dismounted and walked to the door, where he saw an even-featured face, grizzled as it was, with bright gray eyes. The man peered at the scarlet jacket and lowered his rifle. "You're one of those new Northwest Mounted Police," he commented. "But not the one I saw a few weeks back."

"I've replaced him," Fargo said and followed Asa

65

Hoddy into the room, where he saw a sturdy, spacious dwelling with a good stone fireplace and chimney. He saw Asa Hoddy eye him skeptically.

"Another damn fool idea the government's come up with," Asa said with a grunt.

"This one might work," Fargo said as Asa motioned for him to sit down on a leather hassock. "I've come about the Cree. Something damn strange is going on with them," Fargo said.

"That's for sure," Asa Hoddy agreed.

"Tell me what you've seen," Fargo said.

"They've been taking their pelts and skins for sale as usual, only they've been going way downriver to sell them, way past Moose Jaw. I don't know of them selling to any of their usual outlets, not the Hudson Bay posts. None of the independent buyers, not even riverboat drifters. It just doesn't make any sense for them to go way downriver."

"They've been doing more than peddling their pelts. They've been murdering people in real vicious attacks," Fargo said.

"Haven't seen that, but I heard talk of it," Asa said. "That's not like the Cree."

"You heard of any renegade Cree, a band of hotheads out to make trouble?" Fargo queried.

"No, and I would've had wind of that. Maybe it's just part of the times. Canada's changing. There's a new wildness over everything. Maybe the Cree are just caught up in it, too."

"There's something more than that. I'm convinced the people they've attacked were killed because they saw something they shouldn't have seen," Fargo said.

"Then whatever it was I haven't seen it. All I've seen

is the Cree going about their business as usual, except for going way downriver."

"Thanks for your help," Fargo said. "I'd appreciate you keeping your eyes and ears open."

"Count on it. You stop by anytime," Asa said. He watched Fargo leave the hut, the pinto at a slow trot. Fargo rode through the night, moving down the hills as his ears took in the night sounds, the soft swish of bats, the click-clack of stag beetles, the faint, brushed sound of a marten moving through the bristlegrass. It was habit born of his acute sensitivity, and as sounds filtered through him he suddenly grew tense. He had picked up another sound, a sound foreign to the night, and his eyes narrowed as the sound took form and became the tinkle of a rein chain. A rider following him, he murmured inwardly. He tuned his ears to the night again and the sound came once more. Another followed, the faint scrape of low branches being moved aside. More than one rider following.

He let the pinto move on unhurriedly and picked up the sound of a third rider. They had followed him from town, waited while he visited with Asa Hoddy, and now were closing in on him. A tight smile touched his lips. They were amateurs, their efforts crude, and he continued to ride on slowly as his ears told him their every move. They had separated, one hanging behind, the other two fanning out to come up on each side of him. Fargo let them close in as they began to draw abreast of him. The third one still hung back, he noted. The first two had come opposite him, and they began to turn to move toward him from both sides. Fargo drew the big Colt as he silently counted off seconds as they came closer and suddenly started to gather speed. He dropped from the Ovaro with his knees half bent and spun as he landed on the ground. His shot caught the first rider as the man came through the trees.

Fargo was already spinning again before the rider hit the ground, his shot splintering the second rider's cheek with an explosion of bone and blood. The third rider came charging up, firing furiously, but Fargo had already ducked under the Ovaro. He hit the ground rolling and stopped against a tree. He fired and heard the third rider curse in pain. But the man sent his horse into a gallop through the heavy tree cover at a speed that risked a broken leg for his horse and a broken neck for himself. Fargo rose as the rider raced away. He holstered the Colt and stepped to the other two figures on the ground. He bent down, searched through their clothes, and came up with two pay stubs, one on each man and both signed by Caleb Barton.

Fargo allowed a grim grunt as he climbed onto the pinto and rode away. The cabin was dark and silent when he reached it, and he undressed and slept at once. He heard Lisette wake with the morning and gave himself another half hour before he rose and dressed. Her hazel eyes were questioning when he finished telling her of the night. "You going to push it down Barton's throat?" she asked.

"Maybe. He'll try to cover his tracks, of course," Fargo said. "Meanwhile, let's see to the Cree. Barton's small fry compared to them." Lisette brought her horse alongside his as he rode from the hills down toward the river, where he swung in alongside the right bank. He had gone perhaps a mile when he drew to a halt, his eyes peering at the shoreline. "Hoofprints, two horses," he muttered. "And over there, moccasin prints, four of them." Eyes narrowing, he peered at a third set of marks, boot marks, and a scraped trail of sand that led to the water.

"Someone was dragged into the river?" Lisette questioned.

"Something or someone," Fargo nodded, and he dismounted, removed his shirt, and let himself sink into the river. He swam underwater, groped his way along, half turned, swam further, and finally had to surface. Drawing another deep breath, he sank downward again. He swam in a tighter circle, and suddenly his hand, moving along the river bottom, touched something. He reached forward and the object turned out to be an arm, a shoulder following. Wrapping his own arm around the appendage, and using the last of his breath, he kicked upward, pulling the body with him. He burst to the surface sputtering, just as it seemed his lungs were ready to explode. Drawing in a drop of breath, he crawled ashore, pulling the figure partly out of the water. He stared down at the figure, who wore a dark, formal jacket and trousers and a shirt with a wing collar. Two sample cases filled with a variety of tools projecting from them had been tied around his neck as a weight.

"A tool salesman," Fargo murmured. "He was sunk to the bottom, where they figured he wouldn't be found for months, at least."

Lisette glanced at the prints in the soil. "The Cree and somebody else or just the Cree using different horses?" she asked. "I guess the question is kind of an echo."

"So's our answer." Fargo snorted grimly as he donned his shirt and swung back onto the Ovaro as the drowned figure began to slide back into the river to once again disappear. "The poor bastard made the same mistake as the others. He came onto something he shouldn't have seen," Fargo said as he rode forward with Lisette. They rode on in silence and saw only a lone canoe with three Cree inside it as they patrolled the river, and finally Fargo drew up at the Danner place, where Caryn came out with Horace.

"I told you Barton was a bad actor," Horace said when Fargo recounted what had happened. "You going after him now?"

"Not now. He'll deny any part in it and I'd guess he'll lay back for a while," Fargo said.

"But he'll try again. He's that kind," Horace said, and Fargo allowed a grim smile.

"I'll be ready," he said as Caryn turned to him.

"You're still tracking down the Cree," she said, and he nodded. Her full lips tightened for an instant, and she came to stand close to him. He smelled the faint but lovely odor of violet-scented orris soap, and she spoke in almost a whisper, her clear blue eyes very round. "I said I wanted to talk to you alone. Can you come back late tonight?" she asked.

"All right," he said.

"Thanks. I'll be waiting," she said, and her hand pressed his arm, a fleeting motion, before she drew back. Horace had become busy with a trapper who arrived pulling two mules, and Fargo waved to him.

"See you soon," he called and moved the Ovaro forward as Lisette fell in behind him. He moved through the hills to the east and managed to stay within glimpse of the river from time to time, but when night fell he had one answer. "It won't be easy finding new trails for Horace," he observed. "The land becomes too dense and hilly when you leave the old routes. I'll strike out due north tomorrow."

"What about the Cree?" Lisette asked.

"We'll patrol the river, first. We'll split up again," he said, and the night was deep when they reached the cabin. "Caryn Danner asked me to visit her. You'll be asleep when I get back," he said.

Lisette swung from her horse and put on the kerosene lamp and in its glow Fargo saw the faint smile edge her lips. "She has eyes for you, that one," Lisette remarked.

"What makes you say that?" Fargo frowned. "Hell, she's not even happy with me."

"It's still so."

"Ridiculous," Fargo said.

"A woman always knows," Lisette said, the enigmatic little smile staying on her lips.

"You're overtired. Get some sleep," Fargo said and sent the pinto into the night. He rode through shortcuts under the moon, and when he reached the Danner spread, the door of the smaller house opened and Caryn came out. She waited for him to dismount and led him inside. A lamp burned low in a modest room, furnished simply with a settee and chairs. He noted a second room back of the first and saw that Caryn wore a white nightgown tied with a red bow at the waist that accentuated the fullness of her breasts.

"Sit down, please," Caryn Danner said, and she slid down on the settee beside him, the lamplight lightening her almost blond hair. "Thanks for coming. I wanted your visit late so Horace would be sure to be asleep. There are things I have to tell you because I believe in you. I believe you want to help Horace.

"That's true."

"That's why you have to hear what I'm going to tell you, Fargo. Horace made it sound as though he had time to wait for you to find a new route for him. He doesn't. When I came here to help him I found out how bad it was. I told him to pack it in and I'd find a new start at something else, but he refused. He said he didn't know how to do anything else and so now he's out of time and money. He's too proud to tell you the truth, but I'm not," Caryn Danner said, and her hands closed over Fargo's. "You have to put aside everything but helping Horace. Forget the Cree, forget being a Mountie, forget everything but finding a new route for Horace."

"That could still take a good while," Fargo said.

"I know. That's why there's no time for anything else. That's why every minute counts," she said. She leaned forward and Fargo felt the softness of her breasts against his hands. "Do this and I'll say thanks in my own way, Fargo," Caryn said.

"That won't figure in," he said and saw her brows lift. "I've nothing against being thanked. I'm not much for being bought."

She slid a slightly rueful smile at him. "Of course. I should have known better," she said, and her arms lifted and suddenly her full lips were against his, softly enveloping him for a long moment. "No thanking, no buying, just wanting," she smiled. "Is that better?"

"Much better," he said as he inwardly thought of Lisette's words and the mysteries of female wisdom.

"I've told you everything, now," Caryn said as she rose. "It's up to you."

"I'll sleep on it," Fargo said. "You've given me a lot to think about and a few surprises along the way."

"Such as?"

"Being as attached to Horace as you are. I know he's your stepfather and you've only been with him for a year," Fargo said.

"I came to know what a really fine person he is," she said. "And I've always been quick to decide about people. But maybe you know that already."

"Maybe." He shrugged and she walked to the door with him, her softly full thigh brushing against his leg. She closed the door quietly, without waiting for him to climb onto the Ovaro, but he caught the small, private smile that touched her lips. He turned the pinto west and rode through the late-night hills. Caryn Danner had been a surprise, not only in her concern for Horace but in a warmth he'd not detected before. Perhaps it was only right to do as she'd pleaded. Helping Horace was the reason that had brought him here in the first place, he pondered as he rode. Perhaps he'd been wrong in thinking he could do more than one thing at a time, and now Horace Danner's plight had a new urgency. He was still turning the questions in his mind when he reached the cabin and saw, in surprise, the lamplight still on.

He dismounted and started toward the cabin when he spied the rifle lying on the ground a few yards from the door. He recognized it as Lisette's, and the frown darkened his brow as he strode into the cabin, his hand already resting atop the Colt at his side. "Lisette," he called, but silence was his only answer. Cursing the wave of coldness that swept through him, he spun and strode outside, where the glow from the lamp let him pick up the small half circle of footprints on the ground, two sets of bootprints, and Lisette's moccasins.

The night blackness swallowed up anything more, but he had seen enough and he swore again silently. There'd be no chance to pick up a trail until dawn, and he strode into the cabin, turned off the lamp, and stretched out in the blackness. Dawn was but a few hours away, he realized with a bitter gratefulness, and he forced himself to snatch precious sleep. With the instinct of the wild, his eyes snapped open as the first pink streaks of the new dawn touched the sky. He was in the saddle as daylight peeled back the night, his lake blue eyes narrowed as he scanned the ground and the tall banks of joe-pye weed beyond.

5

Three horses, one of them Lisette's, he saw as he spurred the Ovaro forward. The two men were keeping her between them, riding on each side of her or in tandem where the paths grew narrow. They had headed northwest and had made little effort to hide their flight as he picked up the trail with ease. Fargo had ridden for some three hours when he reined to a halt to see where they had stopped to rest. The footprints showed where they had tied Lisette to a tree, and he leaned down and ran his fingers over the prints. Not more than three hours old, he estimated as he sent the Ovaro forward again. Black spruce rose up to form a heavy cover, and he followed them through a narrow and twisting deep path when suddenly the sun caught the clear blue of a wide stream.

He saw where the three horses had moved into the stream and he reined to a halt along the nearest bank. There were no hoofprints coming out the other side. They had suddenly decided to grow cautious and move through the wide stream, confident they would throw off any possible pursuers. It was a trick that would have worked with most pursuers, but the Trailsman was not most pursuers. He dismounted, walked to the center of the stream, and knelt down on all fours. Using both hands, he slid his way along the bottom of the stream. There'd be no tracks at the bottom of the swift-moving water, but three horses had passed through. They had to have dislodged and pushed aside the small, smooth rocks that made up part of the streambed. He moved another few feet, halted, and turned back the other way in the water, still sliding his hands slowly, when suddenly he halted. They had come this way, south in the stream, his hands feeling along the thin lines where the small stones had been pushed aside by hooves.

He rose, used a hand motion to call the Ovaro, and slid into the saddle to move carefully downstream. His eyes moved back and forth along both banks until suddenly he saw the three sets of prints emerge from the water, almost a mile downstream. They set off directly across a slope of low brush, and Fargo put the Ovaro into a gallop. Icy apprehension had begun to wrap itself around him. They could have killed Lisette at the cabin, but they hadn't. That wasn't because they planned a kinder fate for her. They plainly had orders to get rid of her someplace else, where she would just disappear. That moment had to be drawing near, Fargo realized, and he raced the pinto after the trail. They had slowed and he was close behind, now, he saw, and they turned sharp west to climb higher into hill country, a terrain that quickly became wild and rugged. Fargo caught sight of one pack of big gray timberwolves, at least three grizzlies, and the unmistakable snarl of a wolverine caught his ears.

The land had grown steeper, with aspen and balsam fir forests affording cover for the caves time had carved from the rock. Fargo slowed as he saw the hoofprints grow closer together, the horses shortening their stride, and then they came to an abrupt halt. Fargo reined to a halt, also, his eyes sweeping the ground to see they had dismounted and taken Lisette on foot up a short, steep slope, and he saw the mouth of the cave. He followed, paused, and saw where the two pairs of bootprints came from the cave and went alongside a line of fir as they returned to the bottom of the slope. He knelt down and ran his fingers over the prints. They were still clean and firm. They weren't much over ten minutes old, he guessed as, Colt in hand, he entered the cave in a cautious crouch. He paused, let his eyes adjust to the dank dimness, and he took in the very pungent odor of bear, when suddenly the slender figure came into his sight. He ran forward.

Lisette was conscious, her eyes open, gratitude flooding their hazel depths, but she was gagged and bound, wrists and ankles tied to a heavy length of broken tree branch. He took the gag from her mouth, and Lisette's voice echoed the flood of relief in her eyes. "Oh, God," she breathed. "Oh, God, you found me." Fargo took in the ropes that bound her and saw she could never have undone them, nor would have had the strength to move the piece of tree. Using his throwing knife, he cut through the ropes, and she was in his arms, clinging to him until he rose to his feet with her.

"What happened?" he asked.

"One of them came to the cabin. I answered holding my rifle. He told me your horse had fallen and you needed help and you sent him to get me," she said. "I put down my rifle and went to get my horse. The other one came up from behind and grabbed me. Then they both took me. I never had a chance."

Her face showed the strain, but there were no tears, he noted. "They say anything else to you?" he asked.

"Not another word after that, not another damn word. They just took me and we rode," Lisette said.

"They left you for the wolves and grizzlies or maybe a hungry wolverine. By night they'd have all started coming around," Fargo said. "One or the other would've torn into you." He led her from the cave, where she halted, her eyes sweeping the scene.

"They took my horse with them," she said.

"Very thorough. Very professional. I want them. I'm going after them. They're not that far ahead," Fargo said and drew the big Henry rifle from its saddle case. "Keep this with you and wait here. I'll be back before dark."

"Be careful and be sure you come back," Lisette said, taking the rifle as he swung onto the Ovaro and sent the horse into a fast canter. He picked up the trail of the three horses as the two riders led Lisette's mount behind them. They weren't hurrying, he saw, and his smile held a grim satisfaction. Overconfidence was one more mistake they'd pay for, he vowed, and kept the Ovaro racing up a slope where their tracks moved across an open area. He had crossed the top of the slope when he caught sight of the two horsemen. They were still pulling Lisette's mount behind them, obviously bent on selling the horse when they reached a town.

They rode between the stands of white spruce, and Fargo put the Ovaro into an all-out gallop, aware there was no way to sneak up on his quarry. He was closing distance fast when they heard him, both turning in their saddles at once, and he saw the moment of surprise in their faces. They dropped the reins of Lisette's horse, went into a gallop, and swerved sharply and raced into

78

one of the thick spruce forests. Fargo followed but sent the Ovaro a dozen yards to the left of the horsemen, and he glimpsed the two riders as he raced past them through the forest, letting the Ovaro's nimble-footed power swerve through the trees while hardly slowing. Fargo knew the two men saw flashes of him as he went by, and he knew they'd be alarmed, uncertain of his maneuvers. They were peering hard through the thick spruce, trying to glimpse him again, when Fargo yanked the Ovaro into a sharp turn and cut through the trees directly ahead of the two men.

He reined the horse to a sharp halt, stood up in the stirrups, and wrapped his arms around the thick branch of a stout spruce. Pulling himself up, he flattened his body along the branch as he drew his Colt from its holster. He grinned in satisfaction as the two riders reacted exactly as he expected they would. When they heard the sound of his horse suddenly break off, they knew he had come to a stop, and they did the same thing at once. They dropped from their saddles, certain he had hit the ground to pick them off, and Fargo heard them carefully begin to search through the spruce. They were being very cautious, pausing with each step to peer forward and on both sides, trying to draw a bead on him by eye or ear.

Hardly breathing, Fargo stayed flattened atop the branch, hidden in the dark green needles that rested almost atop each other. Straining his ears, he caught the faint sound of their cautious steps, the hushed pressure of the carpet of spruce needles, when suddenly he caught a glimpse of one half-crouched figure. The man halted, half hidden behind the tree trunk, and then slid forward. Fargo waited until he glimpsed the second figure, a dozen feet to the side. Both had their guns out, their eyes sweeping the ground and the tree trunks. Fargo's eyes narrowed on the first figure. He needed only one alive and able to talk and his finger tightened on the trigger. They had left Lisette to be torn apart, and he had no compunctions about what he had to do. But he had to be ready to do more than shoot. His position would be revealed the minute he fired. The man started to dart across the narrow space to the next tree, and the big Colt exploded.

The man's body arched backwards as the bullet tore through him, but Fargo was already dropping from the tree branch. He hit the ground as the second man blasted a volley of shots upward at the branch, took the impact of the fall on his side, and rolled between two trees, where he dived behind one of the trunks as the man's two shots slammed into the ground. He rose on one knee, stayed behind the trunk, and heard the man reloading behind a tree almost opposite from him. "You've one chance to stay alive," Fargo called out. "Talk and you can walk. I want answers."

The man's answer was a shot that tore into the ash brown bark a half inch from where Fargo waited, followed by the sound of footsteps plunging through the brush. Stepping from behind the tree, Fargo glimpsed the man darting through the trees to where his horse waited. He let another dozen seconds go by as the man vanished for a moment behind a branch and then reappeared, pulling himself into the saddle. Fargo fired, a single shot aimed low, and the man clutched at his thigh with a curse as he toppled from the horse. Fargo ran forward, the Colt still raised, the man on both knees on the ground, his thigh growing red. "Drop the gun. Don't be a

80

damn fool," Fargo said, and the man looked up, lips pulled back in pain. But he let the gun fall from his hand as he slumped down onto the ground, holding his wounded leg out straight.

Fargo lowered the Colt and walked to the man, who had a thin mustache on a broad face that glowered up at him. "Talk. Who hired you?" Fargo bit out.

"Back pocket. Piece of paper," the man muttered.

Fargo dropped to one knee and began to reach into the man's hip pocket. "Easy, my leg hurts real bad," the man said and half turned from Fargo to make it easier for him to reach his hip pocket. Fargo had begun to slide his hand into the pocket when he caught the sudden movement of the man's arm, glanced up, and cursed as he saw the pistol drop into the man's hand from inside his shirt, a Frank Wesson double-barreled derringer. He flung himself sideways, but the derringer fired, only inches from his face. Fargo swore. The bullets missed, but the yellow flashes blinded him at point-blank range. He fell backward, rolled, and rubbed his eyes frantically with his left hand while he held on to the Colt with the other. He shook his head and the blinding light faded, the world began to take shape, and became the man crawling across the ground to his gun.

Lying on his stomach, dragging his wounded leg behind, the man closed his hand around the gun. He started to bring the pistol up and Fargo cursed as he fired the Colt. The man's chest erupted in a cascade of bone and blood and his body shuddered for almost a minute before he lay still, facedown in a quickly spreading red stain. "Shit," Fargo snapped as he pushed to his feet. "No answers. No goddamn answers." He strode to where the man's horse waited, opened the saddlebag, and rummaged through it and felt his hand close around a thick packet. He pulled it out to stare down at the sheaf of bills and saw there was at least a thousand dollars in Dominion of Canada currency. He strode to the second horse and yanked the saddlebag open to find another packet of bills. They were both answers of a kind, payment for services rendered. Both packets of bills were neatly and securely bound in lengths of narrow black yarn, the kind used in crocheting. He swore again, walked to the Ovaro, and put the two packets of bills into his own saddlebag, gathered Lisette's horse, and swung onto the Ovaro.

He retraced his steps and in the warm sun of the midafternoon he found Lisette waiting where he'd left her, the big Henry clutched firmly in her hands. He swung to the ground, and she was against him at once, holding herself to him for a long moment that needed no words. "We'll talk while we ride," he said, and she gave him back the rifle and swung onto her horse. He set a slow pace down the slope as Lisette rode beside him. "They were paid two thousand in Dominion money. I have it in my saddlebag," he told her.

"Their real target was you, of course, to make it so that whatever you do you'll have to do alone," Lisette said.

"With a lot less chance of success." Fargo nodded.

"It had to be Caleb Barton again," she said.

"Yes, but I'm surprised," Fargo murmured.

"Why?"

"I didn't expect he'd move again so quickly, and I figured him for the kind who'd go on using his own men. These two were a different stripe, smarter and more efficient," Fargo said.

"He smartened up. He realized his oafs couldn't do it," Lisette said with a sniff.

"I'm still surprised," Fargo said as he topped a slope to come upon a small, jewel-like lake, sparkling in the late-afternoon sun. Lisette steered her horse to the water's edge and swung to the ground.

"I feel soiled, outside and in," she said as she stepped to the water. She shed her moccasins and slowly began to unbutton the leather vest, wriggling her shoulders to cast it off. The vest dropped to the ground and Fargo took in beautifully smooth skin, a faint touch of red-tan in its hue, square shoulders, and breasts that, while a little shallow, curved beautifully at the bottoms with flat, deep pink nipples on small areolas of matching pink. Her hand moved to the deerhide skirt and suddenly it was at her feet and she was standing beautifully naked before him. He saw narrow hips, a small waist, and a flat, almost concave midsection, a slender, lithe shape with a curly black triangle so small it seemed virginal. Long, slender legs carried just enough flesh on their thighs to avoid being skinny.

The hazel eyes stayed on him for another moment, her handsome face expressionless, and then she turned and walked into the lake, flat, tightly firm rear hardly moving. He watched her sink up to her waist in the water when she turned again, softly curved breasts just touching the top of the water, her face still expressionless. "You joining me?" she asked.

"Why not?" Fargo answered as he began to unbutton the scarlet jacket. Lisette had sunk underwater and come up again by the time he had stripped down. She lay floating on her back, little beads of water glistening on the slightly shallow breasts, and she turned and went underwater again as he swam out to her. He let the cool, clean water wash him down, dived on his own, surfaced, and found her only inches away. Her arms rose from the water, encircled his neck, and suddenly her lips were on his, sweet wetness, clinging, making tiny, tremulous motions. His hand rose, came around one of the shallow breasts. She made a soft sighing sound.

He found the lake bottom, stood, picked her up into his arms, and stepped out of the water. A wide, soft bank of nut moss spread from the lakeshore, and he lay down on it with her and let his eyes take in the lithe loveliness of her body, one long leg half raised, her almost concave abdomen glisteningly inviting. His mouth closed over hers, pulling, pushing with his tongue, and Lisette's lips responded at once. "Yes," she breathed. "Yes." He moved his lips slowly down her neck, pioneering a soft path, down across the ledge of her collarbone and then closing around one shallow breast. His tongue circled the deep pink tip, and his lips closed gently around it, drew on it, pulled, sucked, and he felt the flat nipple gather itself, rise, find a new shape. "Oh, yes . . . ah . . . aaaaaah," Lisette breathed and her shoulders half lifted, pressing herself upward against his mouth.

His hand cupped her other breast, then traced its own path slowly down her narrow waist, circled the elliptical little indentation, and let his lips follow. Lisette's body began to slowly writhe, shoulders, waist, hips, all moving in a serpentine motion. His hand moved across the wet nap, flattened even smaller with dampness, and he felt the round curve of her Venus mound, provocative in its little-girl bareness. His hand moved downward to the tip of the tiny triangle and suddenly he felt a new wetness, warmer, viscid, exciting. He touched the silky soft moist flesh, and Lisette suddenly half screamed, and her long, lithe thighs fell open and his hand was upon the trembling lips. "*Mon Dieu* . . . ah, ah . . . ah *mon Dieu*," she gasped, and he felt the almost bare mound push up against him as her hips lifted. He pressed deeper, and Lisette's torso twisted and writhed in the serpentine motion, the flesh entreating, all contained calm swept away. Lisette's body pressed itself against him, and she rubbed her breasts up and down. He felt her hands sliding along his torso. "Yes, oh, oh . . . ooooooh," she whispered, and as her hand found his wildly throbbing warmth, fingers closing around him, she screamed, low, deep, throaty screams, and the slender thighs were opening for him. "Take me . . . God, take me," he heard her breathy gasp.

He moved, halted, his warmth against the edge of the moist portal, and Lisette's low, throaty screams became a deep moan, growing, deepening, rising, falling as he held there, let her tremble against him as her wanting spiraled. Finally, with a wild cry, she flung herself against him and he slid forward, feeling his own surge of pleasure as she engulfed him in her sweet vise. She moved with him, strong, lithe legs sliding up and down against his buttocks, his back, the deep pink nipples erect in his mouth, immersed in the senses as completely as she had been in the lake. He felt her suddenly grow tense, her wild slidings change, become sudden pumping, and he cried out aloud at the ecstacy of her contractions around him. He felt himself spiral with her, his arms encircling her, his face pressed against the slightly shallow breasts.

"Now, now, oh, now . . . aaaaaagh," Lisette flung out in a throaty roar, and he exploded with her, swept up with her and by her, ecstasy exchanged, senses engulfing senses until suddenly the wild trembling spiraled away, too soon yet almost not soon enough. He lay with her, inside her, feeling her warmth and the murmured sighs of the body as she clutched him against her, pleasure reluctant to unravel. Finally she grew limp against him and he half turned, rolled onto his side, and let his eyes take in the lithe beauty of her. His hand rested against the tiny triangle as her eyes opened, and she peered at him with a very wise smile edging her lips. "I knew it would be like this with you," she murmured. "I knew from the very beginning."

"Did you know it would happen?" he asked.

"No," she said. "I did not know that."

"Did you hope it would?" he slid at her.

"Probably," she said. "The body sets its own rules, its own hopes."

He sat up and pulled her with him. There was only another hour of daylight left. "It's time to get back to the cabin. There are still things to talk about."

"Yes, such as your late-night visit to Caryn Danner," Lisette said as she dressed and swung onto her horse. Night came as they rode, and he told her what Caryn had asked of him. She listened and rode in silence until they finally reached the cabin when the moon was high. When he unsaddled the horses and returned to the cabin, she had two bowls of potato soup waiting. Sitting across the small puncheon table from him, she asked the question casually, though he immediately knew there was nothing casual about it. "You going to go along with what she wants you to do?" Lisette pushed at him.

"I didn't know how desperate things were for Horace," Fargo said. "And he is the reason I came here."

Lisette made no reply, her lovely handsomeness veiled by an expressionless mask. "You don't approve," he remarked, and she didn't answer at once. "Sometimes you have to choose," he added, a little defensively.

"What happens to Horace Danner if you can't find him a good, new route or it takes too long?" she asked, finally, another query he knew was deceptively simple.

"He's finished. He'll have to find a new living for himself. I'd guess Caryn will try to help him do that," Fargo answered. Lisette nodded and lapsed into silence again, the hazel eyes still veiled. Fargo finally broke into the silence impatiently. "Go on, say it, whatever you're thinking," he tossed at her.

"I'm thinking about choosing and I'm thinking that not everything has the same importance," she said, and he frowned back. "Choosing ought to be about importances," she said.

"Spell it out," he said.

"The men, women, and children on that wagon train will never find a new living for themselves. They'll never have that chance. Nor will any of the others the Cree have killed, and there'll be more unless these Cree attacks are stopped. There's being discomforted and there's being dead. I don't see there's much choosing in it," she said, her hazel eyes meeting his gaze almost resentfully.

"You don't leave any room, do you?" he said, and her silence answered. "All right, that's how you call it," he offered.

"No, that's how it is," she returned, unwilling to allow any room for compromise. She could use words as knives, he saw, slashing with icy hardness, yet he couldn't close out the truth in them.

"I'll sleep on it," he muttered.

"Not alone," she said, the hazel eyes softening, and he was quick to accept. All her unyieldingness vanished as she lay with him, her naked warmth comforting as well as exciting, and they filled the night with the sounds of pleasure until they finally slept.

When day came he lay awake, and her words flooded back over him. He learned the power and pain of truth that denied compromise. He rose, went to the well, and washed, and he was dressed when she woke. He watched her lovely lithe body as she stretched, breasts lifting with easy grace, and saw her finally focus on him. Her eyes moved up and down his figure, but she said nothing as she went outside to the well to wash. Only when she returned, buttoning the leather vest, did she speak as her glance halted on him again. "Seeing as to what you've decided, I don't think you ought to be wearing that uniform," she said, a hint of reproach in her voice.

"Just helping Horace isn't being a Mountie?" he asked evenly, and her face was set as she nodded. "I sort of felt that way myself," he said with an affable smile. Her eyes stayed fastened on him, narrowing ever so slightly.

"But you're wearing it," she said.

"That's right," he said. Her eyes stayed on him, searching his face, and suddenly her arms were around his neck, her lips pressing his. "You made your point," he said as she drew back.

"Thank you, Fargo," she said.

"Now, there's one thing left," he said and led her outside to saddle the horses. "You're leaving."

"What?" she said, her frown instant.

"Last time was too close. I'm not having another try at

88

killing you to get to me," he said. "And I'll have all to do to watch out for myself."

"No, I'm not leaving," Lisette protested.

"Yes, you are, honey," Fargo said. "It'll be best for both of us. Right now nobody knows you're alive. It'll be assumed the job was done and you're dead. I want to leave it that way. The two thousand dollars was to buy your death. You take it. You earned it. I want you to ride, stay to the back roads. Go to Colonel French in Moose Jaw and lay low there."

"It's not fair," she said. "You'll need me."

"I'll need to be alone, with no one but myself to watch out for," he repeated. "I want you alive and waiting when I'm finished. You see, it's not completely un-selfish."

Her eyes softened, but only for a moment. "It's not right," she murmured.

"I didn't say it was right. I said it was best," he told her. "Now get out of here." She clung to him for a long moment, her lips warm, pressing, enticing, but he finally pulled away, and she swung into the saddle. He put the packet of bills into her saddlebag and watched her ride away, refusing to look back, reproach in the very way she sat her horse. Finally, when she was out of sight, he climbed onto the Ovaro and turned the horse northeast for the Danner place. When he reached the houses that stretched out near the river, he saw Horace beside one of the drying racks that held two pelts when it should have held twenty. Caryn was talking to a man standing near a well-groomed bay stallion. Well dressed in gray twill trousers and a gray jacket with black velvet lapels, the man had a strong face with dark blond hair, a straight nose, wide mouth, and sharp gray eyes. It was a face that exuded a rakish handsomeness, and as Fargo reined to a halt he caught Caryn's quick glance at his scarlet jacket.

"Fargo, this is an old friend of my mother's, Ralph Abernoy," she introduced.

"One of Colonel French's new lawmen, his Northwest Mounted," Abernoy said, his voice hearty. "The colonel's an optimist. That goes for Robertson-Ross and MacDonald and all the others."

"Why's that?" Fargo asked.

"They think they can run the new Canada with a handful of lawmen and a bunch of paper-pushing officials full of stupid rules and regulations." Ralph Abernoy laughed.

"The colonel mentioned you to me. It seems you and some others want a wide open Canada with a few strong men running things," Fargo said.

Abernoy's smile was expansive. "That's right. No interference from bureaucrats and none from the Crown," he said. "But I wish you well, Mountie. You've a hell of a job ahead of you. Good day to you." He turned and strode to his horse, and Caryn went with him. Fargo found Horace coming up to him, his voice low.

"Never liked that man," Horace said. "Of course, Caryn's known him for some years. That's why he drops by whenever he comes this way." Fargo waited till Ralph Abernoy took his leave of Caryn and rode away before he spoke to them both.

"Got some bad news," he said. "Real bad. Lisette's gone. They took her. There's every chance she's dead."

"My God," Horace gasped out. "It had to be Caleb Barton. He'll do anything to make it harder for you to help me."

"Yes, of course," Caryn put in. "It's a terrible thing."

Her eyes went to Fargo, paused on the scarlet jacket again, hardening for an instant as Horace returned to his drying rack, shaking his head in despair.

"I take it you're not going to do what I asked," Caryn said.

"Yes, I am, but my way," Fargo answered.

"You're turning your back on Horace," Caryn said, letting a sadness come into her voice.

"No. I'm just not turning my back on anyone else," Fargo said. "Don't sell me short yet."

Her hand found his and her eyes turned a softer blue. "I don't want to do that. I want to help you, in any way I can, especially now that Lisette's not here. I could ride with you while you search for a new route for Horace. Just tell me and I'll do it," she said.

"I might take you up on that later," he said, and she reached upward and brushed his cheek with her lips.

"Thank you," she whispered and quickly stepped back. "But I'm still disappointed," she said as he swung onto the Ovaro.

"I'll come by when I'm ready," Fargo said and sent the horse into a canter with a wave at Horace. He had formed a rough plan in his mind, the Cree in the morning when it seemed they were most active and scouting for Horace in the afternoon. As it was already noon, he took but a quick glance along the river, saw but one lone canoe, and rode on into the land that stretched to the west. He explored and found nothing, made a wide circle that brought him to Mallardsville, where he stocked his saddlebag with jerky and dried beef strips. As dusk descended, he rode slowly, found a glen, and paused to scan the surrounding terrain before settling in for the night. A little frown touched his brow. With nothing to justify it, he'd had the feeling he was being watched but, again, he saw no movement, no telltale signs he knew how to discern better than an Apache scout.

He finally bedded down and thought about Caleb Barton as he chewed on a length of jerky. Barton had taken him off guard once and really surprised him the second time. If he'd hired someone to follow him it would be the third surprise, Fargo pondered, and realized he still had trouble accepting the attack on Lisette. Caleb Barton didn't seem that wily or that smart. Yet perhaps he had misjudged the man, Fargo admitted. Clinging to the thought, he settled onto his bedroll and slept under the Canadian moon.

6

He was riding the high ground looking down on the river when morning came. He saw only a few lone canoes. When afternoon arrived, he set out to scour the land to the east for Horace, and as he did he scanned the terrain at his rear as the feeling of being watched persisted. But he could spot no movement, no signs of any kind to justify his fears, and he rode on with more annoyance than apprehension. The morning brought no activity to interest him on the river, and soon he was exploring for Horace again.

The days took on a sameness, and he knew the feeling of frustration, first at the Cree and then at the land that refused to offer anything for Horace. Even the sense of being watched remained. Most men would have written it off as nerves or imagination, he knew, but he was subject to neither. There was something, he swore to himself, even if it was only a lone wolf looking for an easy mark. When the nights came, he found a spot to bed down surrounded by dry brush or loose twigs littering the ground, anything that would make it impossible for an intruder to get too close in silence. But no intruder came and the mornings brought him back to his routine.

He was beginning to despair of both of his goals

when, on a warm morning, he suddenly sat upright in the saddle as he spied the line of six canoes paddling furiously upriver, three Cree in each canoe. Squinting, his eyes peered down the river in the direction the Cree had come, and he spotted the thin line of smoke spiraling straight upward in the windless morning. Staying on the high ground, he sent the Ovaro into a gallop, moving down to the river only when he was opposite the smoke which had begun to dissipate. Reining to a halt, he stared at the charred remains of a buckboard and the two bodies in it burned beyond recognition. He moved the Ovaro along the treeline, where it neared the water, and found two sets of hoofprints, both shod. Turning, he raced upriver after the Cree, moving into the thick cover of the high ground, and finally caught up with the six canoes.

They had slowed the pace of their paddling, but were nonetheless keeping up a brisk movement along the winding river. He followed them into the afternoon, saw them take a small tributary that passed Regina, and turn north. He halted when the day began to slide to a close, and he saw the Cree pull to a stop. They lined their canoes one behind the other along the riverbank, and each canoe was heavily laden with pelts, he took note. Climbing from their canoes onto the shore, the Cree quickly settled down and were asleep before the moon was high. Fargo found himself scanning the scene, a tiny furrow digging into his brow which he couldn't explain. But something bothered him, something he couldn't pinpoint. Finally, annoyed with himself, he slept in a glade inside the aspen, once more surrounded by dry brush.

When morning came, he used his canteen to wash, and he watched the Cree take water from the river. Whatever had bothered him during the night clung, but he had no more answers than he'd had then. He was in the saddle when the Cree stepped into their canoes and began to paddle away. Fargo followed and swore at himself as he did. He was having too many unexplained apprehensions, and that made him decidedly unhappy. He had to move down closer to the Cree canoes as the trees grew closer to the water, and he found himself slowing in order to stay behind the canoes. They reached a body of water that widened with a sign along the shore that proclaimed: LANIGAN'S CREEK. Fargo followed, but his lips tightened as he saw his tree cover begin to thin and day starting to slide toward night. The land became open except for high brush and an occasional cluster of paper birches.

Cursing, Fargo slowed still further, and he fell back until he could barely see the six canoes as they continued up the body of water. Hanging back where he wouldn't be spotted, he followed perhaps another half mile when he saw the small collection of buildings along one side of the water, a town that had sprung up bordering Lanigan's Creek. As he watched, the canoes moved toward a stretch of ground that jutted out to form a small protrusion along the riverbank. The Cree sailed their canoes toward the protrusion of land and pulled up alongside it in the gathering darkness, and Fargo swore as he halted the pinto. Only flat, treeless land stretched before him to the town and the stretch of land where the canoes had halted. He slid from the horse and went closer on foot in the night, wondering how close he dared go when he dropped to one knee and froze on the spot. Some eight men appeared to further block his view as they lined up alongside the canoes.

He could see some of the Cree step onto the protrusion of land and carry pelts and skins to the men who had gathered. It quickly become obvious the men were buying everything the Cree had brought, taking their time to examine the pelts, and Fargo wished he could see more, but the men blocked his view from the shore. Finally, the buyers began to move away from the canoes, carrying their purchases. Some of the Cree lingered for a few minutes, but finally they all climbed back into their canoes and began to paddle back the way they had come. Fargo scurried back to his horse and backed the pinto into the edge of the trees as the Cree sailed past.

It had all been a perfectly ordinary transaction, ordinary except for the question that surrounded it and hung in his mind. Why had they gone so far to sell what they could have sold so much closer to their hunting grounds? There were numerous buyers to be found, including Horace, days closer. Yet they had taken this long trip. It made no sense, and it certainly did nothing to explain the savage attacks. Nothing fitted. It all seemed unreal. Only the massacred travelers were very real. Somewhere, there were pieces missing. Without them, he had no answers, only more questions.

His lips drew back in unhappiness, and he saw the Cree find a spot as the moon rose higher. They paddled to the right bank. He watched them pull their canoes to shore and immediately begin to bed down. Fargo moved the Ovaro under a clump of sandbar willows, set out his bedroll, and joined the Indians in sleep. But not before he was aware of again being bothered by that formless irritant he couldn't explain. When the day dawned, he followed the Cree once again as they paddled south, sailed past the connecting tributary to Regina, and turned downriver. Fargo followed more easily, safe in the low hills with their heavy tree cover. From his vantage point, able to see down into the canoes, he saw that two of the Cree carried small soft deerskin pouches. They were probably filled with gold nuggets in payment for the pelts, he surmised.

He found himself riding at a slow pace as the Cree paddled leisurely downriver, and when dusk came they again pulled their canoes from the water and quickly slept. He settled onto his bedroll, his gaze moving across the sleeping Cree, and again he was bothered by something he couldn't give shape or form. Yet the feeling persisted, not unlike a nagging toothache, and he finally pushed it from his mind and let sleep surround him. The Cree continued their leisurely trip downriver when the new day dawned, and Fargo doggedly followed, determined to watch the Cree until they reached their camp. The morning slid through the afternoon, and he found himself sitting straighter in the saddle. The Cree were slowing down still further, and he saw the three in the lead canoe busily scanning the riverbank on both sides. The tree cover suddenly fell away as the river made a long curve, and Fargo drew back to wait for the Indians to move further ahead. He had started to ride into the open when the figure on horseback raced into view. Fargo glimpsed a young boy, probably not more than fourteen, on an overweight gray mare, and when the boy saw him, he wheeled the horse and galloped toward him.

Yanking the mare to a halt, the boy gasped out words, and Fargo saw the red smear along the side of his face. "Help us," the boy said. "You're one of those Mounties. Jeez, you gotta help us."

"Easy now, son. What is it?" Fargo asked, seeing the fright in the boy's eyes.

"It's the Rawsons. They're out to kill my pa and ma and my older brother. They've got everybody trapped inside the house. I got away and went for help," the boy said.

"Where's all this going on?" Fargo asked with a quick glance downriver where the Cree had sailed on.

"Come on, I'll show you," the boy said.

"Hold on, son. I've been tailing some Cree. I can't just let them get away," Fargo said.

"My family's gonna be dead if you don't help us," the boy said. "I thought you Mounties were supposed to help people and keep law and order."

Fargo's lips tightened, and he swore under his breath. He wore the scarlet uniform. He had made a promise to Colonel French to uphold all that it meant. He had no choice. "Let's go. We'll talk while we ride," he said to the boy, who immediately turned the mare northeast up a slope. "What's your name, son?" he asked as he galloped beside the boy.

"Jeb McEvoy,"

"Why are these Rawsons trying to kill your folks?" Fargo queried.

"They want our land. There were five of us families who settled real good grazing land. Nobody wanted to sell to the Rawsons. Three of the other families were found murdered and the Rawsons took over their land. Now our turn's come, it seems."

Fargo slowed the Ovaro to keep pace with the mare, who was plainly getting winded. The boy led the way down an incline, through a cluster of white spruce and alongside a line of chokecherry. Fargo swore silently at the demands of duty. The Cree had long gone their way, perhaps to simply sail back to camp, perhaps with more in mind. He'd never know, now, Fargo swore again, and the volley of gunfire broke off his thoughts. The McEvoy spread came into view and he saw a modest, log-roofed house, barns behind it, and three grazing pens further back.

He also saw the six figures spread in a half circle that let them cover the house from the front and both sides. The attackers fired off another volley, plainly intended to keep those inside pinned down. Fargo took in the situation at once as he cast a quick glance at the sky. The Rawsons had decided to wait for nightfall before rushing the house, and Fargo gestured to a cluster of serviceberry some twenty-five yards to his right.

"Get over there and keep your head down," he said. The boy obeyed, and Fargo let his lips purse in thought for a moment and decided to test out the power of the uniform. He rode forward, into the open toward the six figures, but he kept one hand on the butt of the Colt. Testing was one thing. Foolhardiness was another. The men heard his approach and turned at once, the one in the center a tall, thin figure with a gaunt face and sunken eyes that made him resemble a walking cadaver. Fargo came to a halt as he called out. "Put down those guns," he said. "That's an order."

The man frowned back, and Fargo saw he held a London-made Kerr revolver, a five-shot, double-action piece not known for accurate shooting. "Well, look at this, one of those new Mounties," the man said, the sneer harsh in his voice.

"The guns," Fargo repeated. "Put them down, all of you, in the name of the Northwest Mounted Police."

"Go to hell," the man said. "You got ten seconds to ride out of here or you're a dead lawman."

Fargo saw that the others had half turned, their guns ready to fire. He shrugged his shoulders, an exaggerated motion, defeat in the gesture as he started to ride away. He could feel the boy's overwhelming disappointment. "So much for the Mounties," he heard one of the others call out. Fargo had the Colt in his hand before he wheeled the horse around, his first shot aimed at the gaunt figure. He was a little hasty, the shot high and slightly off, and he saw the man clutch at his shoulder as he let out a cry of pain. Fargo was racing the Ovaro forward as he followed with a sweeping volley of shots, and the others, taken by surprise, first, then automatic reaction, dived for the ground. Fargo reached the service-berry where the boy hid, and he leapt from the saddle.

"Jesus, I'm shot. Get me a damn bandage," he heard the gaunt-faced one cry out and saw two of the others run off to their horses to return tearing off strips of shirt. They helped the gaunt-faced one off to the side while the others continued to cover the house.

"Who'd I shoot?" Fargo asked the boy.

"Mike Rawson," Jeb McEvoy said, and Fargo glanced at the sky. There was not more than fifteen minutes of day left.

"There a rear door to the house?" Fargo asked as he reloaded.

"No, but there are two windows," Jeb said.

"Can I get to the roof?" Fargo queried.

"There's a trapdoor that leads to the roof," the boy said as darkness fell over the land.

"Leave your horse. We'll get inside, first," Fargo said and started for the back of the house in a crouching lope. One of the windows opened as he reached the house, Jeb at his heels, and he saw a young man of about twenty years old waiting for him.

"Pat McEvoy," the young man said and gestured to the older man and the women, who held an old Hawkens plains rifle. "My pa and ma."

"Thanks for coming, Mountie," the man said. "But it looks like they're not paying you much mind."

"They will," Fargo said grimly. "You keep all the lights out in here. They're going to use the darkness to rush you. They'll fire and fire and keep firing, breaking your windows and spraying the place with lead. They lay down a proper barrage and they'll cut down all of you."

"We can try running out the rear windows," the man said.

"There are six of them. They'll have at least one covering the rear," Fargo said. "No, you stay inside. I'm going to turn things around on them. They're going to use the darkness to get up close and start firing their barrage. I'm going to take away that cover. Get a broom," Fargo said to the woman. "Wrap it with all the old rags you can find."

"Coming right up," the woman said. "I don't need light. I know where everything is."

"When she's finished, the rest of you soak the rags with kerosene, grease, oil, whatever you have," Fargo said and discerned Jeb standing beside him as the other two men hurried away. "We've a few minutes. They're still bandaging Mike Rawson's shoulder," Fargo said and waited until the others groped their way back to him with the broomstick swatched in kerosene-soaked rags. "The trapdoor to the roof," Fargo said, and he was shown a ladder built onto one wall of the house. He started up it at once and halted when he reached the top. "At the right moment, I'm going to toss this right in the middle of them. It'll light up the whole damn yard and they won't be able to go near it to kick it aside. They'll be outlined clear as day. That'll be our chance to kick off every damn one of them. Just make sure you shoot fast and straight."

"You can count on that," the oldest McEvoy said, and Fargo pushed the trapdoor open and pulled himself onto the log roof of the house. He lay flat, crawling with the broomstick in one hand until he was a little past the center of the roof. He peered out into the darkness, straining his eyes as he waited, and finally he discerned the shapes beginning to move toward the house. They were spread out, and only the gaunt-faced man carried a revolver, his shoulder bandaged. The others had all taken up rifles. Staying flat atop the roof, Fargo reached down and lighted the rags with a lucifer. He flung the broomstick instantly as the kerosene-soaked rags burst into flame. Then he watched the ball of fire arc through the air and land in the midst of the six attackers. They spun away in surprise and fright as the night lighted up and they were outlined in orange brightness.

A volley of shots exploded from the house, and Fargo saw two of the men go down. His own Colt raised, he fired, and this time Mike Rawson clutched his chest, not his stomach, as he went down. The others, half crouched, started to run, but Fargo saw another go down, struck by at least three bullets. "No more, no more," the last two shouted as they flung themselves facedown on the ground.

"Throw your guns away," Fargo shouted as he rose to one knee. The two men obeyed as they stayed prone on the ground. "Take them," Fargo called out and watched as the McEvoys run from the house. Fargo turned, slid his way back across the roof to the trapdoor, and clambered down the ladder. When he emerged from the house, the McEvoys had the two men already trussed with rope, the rags beginning to burn down. The elder McEvoy came to him and thrust out his hand.

"Jack McEvoy," he said. "We owe you, Mountie. This was all your doing. You going to take these two in, now?"

Fargo pondered for a moment. The Cree were long gone, but there was still a trail to follow and answers to find. He didn't want to go all the way out of his way back to Moose Jaw. "I've unfinished business. I'd like you to take them in for me," he said. "See Colonel French and tell him you've brought them in for Mounted Police Officer Skye Fargo. Then tell him the rest of your story. He'll take it from there."

"Whatever you want, Fargo," Jake McEvoy said.

"Much obliged. Now I'll be getting back to pick up a trail," Fargo said and strode to the Ovaro. The McEvoys were hauling their two prisoners back into the house as he rode off in the darkness. He cut back across the hills to the west and finally came in sight of the river. The moon was sliding close to a midnight sky as Fargo turned south, following the path of the river. Almost another two hours had passed when he came onto the Danner spread, the buildings darkened and silent, and he was in the shadow of a large sandbar willow when he yanked the Ovaro to a halt. A figure moved on foot, in a crouch, across the land toward the smaller house, Caryn's house, and Fargo frowned as he saw the figure wore only a breechclout, moccasins, and a wrist gauntlet.

Glancing at the house, Fargo saw that the window was wide open, the Cree making directly for it. Sliding noiselessly from the saddle, Fargo dropped into his own crouch as he began to cut across the ground toward the Cree. Perhaps luck had suddenly turned his way, he told himself as excitement spiraled through him. This was a Cree prowling the night who decided to take advantage of a window left open for air in the warm night. But a Cree, any Cree, could perhaps provide some of the answers he wanted. The Indian was concentrating on the open window, and he was only a few feet from it when he felt Fargo's presence and spun around. Thin, with a muscular body, Fargo saw the Cree immediately rise on the balls of his feet, his crouch now a crouch of attack. With a quick motion, the Indian pulled a hunting knife from alongside his breechclout and came forward at once.

Fargo kept the Colt in its holster as he moved in a sideways circle, his eyes on the Indian's hands and wrists. When the Cree's wrists tightened, Fargo ducked away and the swiping blow from the knife missed its mark. But the Cree was quick-footed, and he danced forward with fast, slicing blows. Fargo found himself eluding the jagged blade by a hair's breadth as he sidestepped and twisted. Pausing, the Indian gathered himself and came forward again, this time with a blow that went upward, and Fargo barely pulled his head back in time. But the blow left the Cree off balance, and Fargo sent a hooking left upward that crashed into the man's jaw. The Indian went down, on all fours, and Fargo's kick landed in his ribs, and he uttered a loud grunt of pain as he fell sideways. Fargo leapt at him and, midway through the leap, saw that he had been too hasty. The Cree delivered a slashing blow from half on his back, and Fargo had to fling himself to the side to avoid his abdomen being sliced open.

He hit the ground, rolled, and came up on his feet as the Cree charged again, a bellow escaping his pulled-back lips. Counting off split seconds, Fargo let the Indian seem to slam into him, the knife thrust forward, when at the last moment he dropped down and caught the Cree across the belly with his shoulder. The knife scraped along Fargo's hair, but the Cree flew in a half-somersault as Fargo lifted and sent him flying. The Cree hit the ground, and Fargo was at him instantly, closing one hand around the man's knife wrist as he brought his forearm down hard on the man's throat. The Indian gagged in pain and his knees came up in a reflex action. Fargo twisted the wrist and the man's hand came open, the knife falling from it. Releasing the wrist, Fargo sent the knife skittering sideways with a blow of his hand, only to feel a hand yanking him by the hair.

Fargo's head was pulled sideways, and before he could bring a blow to the Cree's abdomen, the man kicked him in the groin, the blow not full yet hard enough. Fargo rolled sideways, shook off the sharp pain, and rose in time to see the Indian diving for the knife on the ground. With a roar of rage, the Indian closed his hand around the knife, spun, and flung himself at his foe, thrusting forward with the blade. Somehow, Fargo managed to twist away so he could feel the knife scrape along his ribs. He stuck out one foot and the Indian tripped, fell forward, and regained his balance to try and spin. But Fargo's roundhouse right caught him on the jaw and he went backward and down. He hit the ground hard, the knife again jarred from his grip.

This time Fargo's kick sent the knife almost to the side of the house, and his blow caught the Indian as he tried to rise. The man fell backward again, rolled, and roared as he tried to close his hands around Fargo's throat. Fargo broke the man's attempt with his arms, ducked low to come up underneath the Cree, and he sent the Indian flying through the air to hit the ground with a resounding thud. The Cree's eyes were glazed, but he started to rise, and Fargo was about to step forward to deliver a crashing blow when the night exploded. With a curse of dismay, Fargo saw the Indian's chest erupt in a shower of red, and he whirled to see Caryn at the open window, the rifle in her hands. "Shit," Fargo burst out.

"It was the first clear shot I could get," Caryn said.

"Ah, shit," Fargo said again, glancing at the lifeless form of the Cree.

"I thought he was going to come at you again," Caryn said, lowering the rifle. She left the window and emerged from the door to press herself into his arms. "The sound of the fight woke me. God, I thought he was going to kill you."

"I could've used my Colt at any time," Fargo said. "I wanted him alive."

"I didn't think of that. I just saw the fight and couldn't get a clear shot till now," Caryn said and looked apologetically up at him as she stayed in his arms.

"You meant well," Fargo said, his arm around her, and he felt the soft roundness of her through the silk night-gown. "I didn't mean to sound ungrateful."

She stayed against him, clinging to him, as he heard the door to the main house open. Horace ran out, wearing only trousers, clutching the Winchester to him. Fargo saw another man step from a shack to the rear. "Everything's under control," Fargo said. "Caryn had an unexpected visitor."

"Luckily, Fargo happened to be passing by," Caryn said.

"That's for damn sure," Horace said, staring at the slain figure.

"I'll take care of him," Fargo said, and Horace nodded gratefully as he returned to the house. Fargo felt Caryn's arm link into his, and she led him to her place, where, inside the doorway, her breasts came against him as her lips found his. The touch of her tongue came to him, sweetly wet, and his mouth opened for her.

"Oh, God, Fargo, I can't fight this off any longer. Stay with me," Caryn whispered. Fargo pulled back, but only with a real effort. He still wanted to be at the Cree camp come dawn, just to see for himself.

"I can't, not tonight," he said, surprised at his own self-discipline.

"Forget the Cree. You've done all you can do," Caryn said.

"Maybe not," Fargo said, and her arms were around his neck, her eyes imploring.

"Come back. Make me a part of whatever you're doing," she said. "For Horace or for anyone. That's what I want now."

"I'll be back, I promise."

"When?"

"Soon as I can, maybe tomorrow," Fargo told her, and she walked outside to the Ovaro with him. "I'd say keep your window closed at night from now on, until this Cree business is finished. You might not be so lucky next time."

"I know," Caryn said, and she kissed him again before

he climbed into the saddle. Fargo flung his lariat around the Indian's neck and let the Ovaro drag him to the river's edge. Loosening the rope, Fargo leaned down, pushed the Cree into the river, and waited a few minutes for the man to be swept downriver on a slow current. Why had the lone Cree been prowling the night, Fargo wondered. Had he been on some special mission? If so, was it connected to those in the six canoes? Or had he been simply an outsider, a loner apart from the tribe? It was not usual, yet it sometimes happened. Whatever his reasons, his detour to enter Caryn's window had back-fired on him. Fargo moved the Ovaro forward and up into the hill country and felt the weariness pulling on him.

By the time dawn swept the sky, he was thoroughly fatigued, and he halted where he could look down on the Cree main camp. Still asleep, the camp was a model of ordinariness, nothing out of place, figures sleeping in and out of teepees, nothing different or unusual, canoes pulled ashore in neat rows. It was as ordinary a picture as the sale of the pelts had been, and Fargo felt a tremendous sense of frustration as he shed clothes and lay down to sleep in a high glade of chokecherry. When he woke some hours later, the camp below was busy, and he watched new skins and furs being prepared by the women and children while the men worked on making new arrows and adjusting bows. Fargo used his canteen to wash, and he swore softly to himself as, once again, he had the distinct feeling that he was being watched. If Caleb Barton, satisfied that he'd gotten rid of Lisette, had set another hired killer after him, why hadn't the man made his move by now, Fargo wondered. He hadn't followed him on the long trek upriver, Fargo was certain.

He hadn't felt the presence of other eyes then, and he would have, he murmured to himself.

Finding a stand of wild pears, Fargo breakfasted and let his eyes slowly sweep the nearby high hills, and his survey paused at a small break in the greenery of a nearby ridge. With a quick glance down at the Cree camp, Fargo moved the Ovaro slowly through the trees, wandering his way carefully, watching the spot on the ridge. As he drew closer, he saw a small glen of white spruce, and his hand rested on the butt of the Colt until he drew to a halt at the edge of the half circle. He scanned the ground in the glen, a perfect spot for someone to bed down and keep watch. But there were no marks, no footprints, no hoofprints, no spot where the grass had been flattened by someone sleeping. No one had been there. Or so the ordinary observer would have concluded. But Fargo allowed a tight smile as he dismounted and knelt on the ground, his hands slowly moving across the grass.

Somebody had been here, spent the night here, someone clever and good at his job. Prints had been obliterated and the grass that had been pressed down by someone sleeping on it had carefully been brushed back and up. Only the extraordinary tracking wisdom of the Trailsman saw that the blades of grass, where they entered the ground, had been bent backward and forward again. They stood upright, but they were bent and weakened at the roots, his fingers finding their telltale softness. Fargo straightened up and climbed into the saddle.

His sixth sense hadn't led him astray, and that was always gratifying. He'd continue to keep his guard up, but now he had bigger fish to fry. He rode downward and back to where he could watch the Cree camp, and when he came in sight of it he felt his brow lift. The Cree were almost finished loading six canoes with furs and hides, working quickly, and Fargo rode closer before reining up in a clump of aspen. He waited until they pulled their canoes into the water and began to paddle upriver. Following as close as he dared, he saw they were moving quickly, paddling with long strokes. It was perhaps a few miles further as he trailed the six canoes when he saw the horsemen suddenly appear from inside the trees near the shoreline, six Cree on their ponies and two white men on sturdy Morgans. The six canoes immediately veered toward the bank to meet the eight riders.

Fargo followed, a frown cutting across his brow as he saw the canoes begin to touch the bank. All his attention concentrated on the scene unfolding before him, he was taken completely by surprise when the high-pitched, half-hissed scream split the air. The Ovaro leapt high and bolted forward in an automatic and natural reaction. Fargo spun as he gripped the saddle horn and saw the big, furred form sail out of the nearby tree, a big Canadian lynx, almost the size of a small mountain lion. The Ovaro still lunged, and Fargo let the Ovaro whirl in the half circle before leaning forward to bring it under control, one hand stroking the jet black neck. But his eyes went to the horsemen, and he cursed softly. They had seen him and they were already streaking for him.

But only the six Cree, he noted, coming fast and spreading out. He sent the Ovaro lunging through the trees. It was past time for trying to be stealthy, and he let the horse crash through the brush. He drew the big Henry from its saddle case as he spotted two of the Cree coming toward him at his right, another two moving to the left, and the third due racing up behind. Two had rifles, he saw, the rest bows. Staying in the saddle, letting the Ovaro dodge its own way through the trees, he raised the rifle, waited, and saw one of the two at his right come into sight again between two trees. He fired and with a short cry, the Indian toppled from his pony. The one with him tried to whirl his pony around before coming into view between the trees, but he was too late. Fargo's second shot sent him flying across his mount's withers before he fell to the ground. Fargo immediately flattened himself across the Ovaro's neck, and two arrows passed, but inches over his head. He swerved the horse behind a tree, pulled up hard, and leapt to the ground, landing on both feet with the Henry in his hands.

The two Cree coming in from the left tried to pull up, but Fargo's shot caught one full in the chest, and the man doubled over as he went down, his rifle falling from his hands. The Cree beside him dived from his horse, hitting the ground on his side and rolling at once. He came up on his knees to fire, but his horse had kept running, leaving him totally exposed. Fargo's shot caught him full on, and the man half spun as he collapsed to the ground. Fargo flung himself behind a tree as he glimpsed the two Cree who had come up from the rear leap from their ponies. Both vanished into the brush and low branches and froze in silence.

Fargo put down the rifle and drew the Colt, aware that he'd need the maneuverability of the handgun over the rifle. He listened and it only took moments. The two Cree were not disposed to play the waiting game, and he heard them move, swift, darting motions, again aimed at putting him in between. He cursed inwardly. The unhesitating quickness of their motions told him they had spotted the tree he'd taken refuge behind. Flattening himself on the ground, he began to push his way backward from the tree, moving slowly and silently. As he crawled backward on his belly, he could see the shapes of the two Cree as they flanked the tree, but not clearly enough for a good shot. He was still inching backward, peering out in front of him, as he saw the one Cree shoot two arrows just past the base of the tree and the other Indian fire three shots from his rifle into the same spot.

They waited for Fargo to fall out into the open, at least wounded, and when nothing happened they stepped out from behind their cover, ready to fire again. Finally they realized their target wasn't there. Fargo had already crawled a dozen yards back under the trees, but the two Cree were still too well hidden by low branches. A shot that missed would spell his finish as it revealed his position, and he held his fire and took the moment to crawl another two feet back. The two Cree crouched, sweeping the trees for any sign of him, and then Fargo heard one bark out words, excitement plain in his voice. Fargo caught a glimpse of his arm as he gestured and knew the Cree had spotted the marks where he'd crawled backward.

They were on their feet, darting forward, but they had separated again to come at him from both sides, and Fargo cursed. To bring down one would be a pyrrhic victory, as the other would surely hit his target. Fargo rose to one knee. His only chance was to stop them from working in unison, and that meant to make them move, give chase, make mistakes. He turned and ran, making no attempt to be silent, and he heard the two Cree shout as they immediately started after him. He sprang from tree to tree, zig zagged, and almost doubled back. He became a darting, dashing, quicksilver form. He heard one of the Cree let fly two shots, neither terribly close, and then he suddenly skidded to a halt as he whirled and fired as the figure came before him.

The Cree cursed in pain as he went down, a sound that quickly became a death rattle, but Fargo was running, in a circle this time, darting and scuttling again, and he saw the second Cree trying to get a bead on him, pausing, firing, missing. Fargo's shot came as he dropped to one knee, and the arrow slammed into the tree trunk over his head. He saw the Cree pitch forward onto his face and lay still. Fargo pushed to his feet, drew a deep breath, and whistled softly. The pinto appeared in but a few moments, and Fargo swung onto the horse and rode downhill slowly, his eyes sweeping the thick tree cover ahead of him, unwilling to risk any more unpleasant surprises.

But the river came into view and the riverbank was empty of everything but the sandbar willows and the flowing waters that lapped the shore. Fargo rode to a halt along the bank, his glance peering into the distance where he saw the six canoes were but tiny specks on the river. He sat quietly in the saddle and let events crystallize in his mind and his thoughts take on new meanings. One of his conclusions had been confirmed. He had almost been another victim, following in the footsteps of those others who had stumbled onto something they shouldn't have witnessed.

It seemed a meeting had been about to take place. But a meeting to do what? He grimaced. The questions still danced in his head without answers. And again, the Cree were paddling on to sell their pelts. It still didn't fit, none of it. Had the meeting taken place, he wondered. His battle with the six Cree on horseback had taken long enough. Though this time he had managed to stay alive, unlike the others who'd been at the wrong place at the wrong time. But the question leapt inside him again. A meeting to do what? Deciding that further speculation was futile, he put the Ovaro into a fast canter and slowly drew closer to the six canoes. He kept to the tree cover of the high ground, and when he was riding abreast of the canoes he peered down into each one. Nothing had changed. Nothing was different, and he couldn't help feeling a sense of unreality as he watched the canoes vigorously paddle upriver.

He slowed and dropped back to keep safely out of sight. He would follow to see if they again took the long trip to the little town beside Lanigan's Creek. When the day finally lowered itself to the dusk, he watched as the six canoes turned to the riverbank and came to a halt. The Cree braves brought their vessels to the edge of the bank and climbed ashore to eat something that looked like pemmican, before stretching out with the darkness of night. The moon rose, and Fargo finished his own dried beef strip as he set out his bedroll. He looked down at the sleeping Cree for a few minutes longer, and the bothersome nagging came to him again, that undefined, elusive feeling that something was wrong.

It was as though he were seeing something, yet not seeing it, and he swore softly as he scanned the scene again, only to come up with the same frustrating result. He lay back and closed his eyes to sleep, aware that the persistent, irritating canker would cling, pushing at his unconscious even as he slept. But he drew sleep around himself, calling on determination and tiredness, and the moon had passed the midnight mark on its way across the night sky when he suddenly sat bolt upright. His eyes, open wide, were staring down at the sleeping Cree below. "That's it. Goddamn, that's it," he whispered as the thought spun through his head, the undefined suddenly defined, the subconscious exploding away the clutter of the conscious mind. Fargo's eyes stayed riveted on the six canoes that were moored by rawhide strips at the edge of the riverbank. But the Cree, as did most Indian tribes, always drew their canoes onshore for the night. There was more, he realized, as his thoughts took form, one now triggering the other. He heard his voice, whispering, as though he needed to reaffirm the realization that had danced out of his conscious reach for the past days and nights.

"They pulled their canoes onshore when they made the trip back to camp," he murmured. "But not when they were on the way to sell their pelts. Why, dammit? The pelts couldn't be that damn heavy." He lapsed into silence as his eyes stayed on the canoes below, and finally he lowered himself back to the bedroll. They hadn't pulled the canoes ashore when they reached the town at Lanigan's Creek, either, he frowned. Maybe the answer to a lot of things lay at the shore of Lanigan's Creek. He frowned, and he began to form his own plans before he returned to sleep.

7

Fargo watched the Cree as they paddled upriver with the morning sun, but this time he rode ahead of them as he stayed in the trees. He put more space between himself and the six canoes until he was finally almost out of sight of them. But he slowed to watch as the turn north came, and he waited to make certain they did so. When they did, he rode on again, keeping ahead, and when the day began to drift toward an end he remembered the long stretch of open land that had kept him at a distance when they reached Lanigan's Creek. He crossed the open space so that when the canoes reached the village he'd be ahead of them and the houses.

Reaching the houses, he slowed and let the Ovaro move casually through the town, which, he took note, was made mostly of storage buildings, wagon yards, a small, shoddy-looking outfit that had the word "saloon" hung over the entrance, and a jumbled collection of sheds and huts he couldn't really see clearly without getting closer. Some of the men in the town noted his uniform, he saw, more with curiosity than anything else, and he was nearing the last of the buildings when two men came from behind a storage shed, one riding a well-groomed bay stallion.

"Now, this is a surprise," he heard the hearty voice say, and he saw Ralph Abernoy's handsome face come to a halt before him. "I thought your territory was down around the Danner place," the man said.

"No, I cover a lot more than that," Fargo said.

"What brings you way up here?" Abernoy asked, his smile still affably expansive.

"Just patrolling," Fargo answered. "And, as I'm sure you know, I'm looking for a new route for Horace."

"Yes, I know."

"Didn't expect to see you up this way," Fargo put in.

"Some associates of mine wanted to meet with me. They've ideas about maybe building a haulage line from here north. Can't really see it myself," Abernoy said, and Fargo touched the brim of his hat with two fingers.

"Good luck. I'm going on north further," he said and moved the pinto forward. He rode on, beyond the last of the town, and kept going until he was out of sight of the buildings before he circled and doubled backward. Abernoy had been an unexpected distraction when he hadn't any time to spare, and, his lips a thin line, Fargo saw the dusk quickly gathering. He rode almost back to the edge of town, carefully scanning the crowds, but Abernoy had apparently gone on and moving the Ovaro behind the back wall of a warehouse-style structure, Fargo began to shed his clothes. When he was down to his underwear, he strode the few feet to the water and lowered himself into the river.

He treaded water as he peered down the river and saw the six canoes come into sight; they were moving toward him and the protrusion of land along the right bank. Fargo sank down and swam underwater to the opposite bank where he emerged and, only the top of his head above water, watched the six canoes move alongside the stretch of land as they had before. But this time he had a view of them denied to him before, and he watched the line of men come down to the shore to examine the pelts the Cree had brought. But as he watched, two men appeared, on the side away from the shore. They sank into the water and moved along the line of canoes, and Fargo felt the frown digging deeper into his brow as the two men reached under the first canoe and came up with a flat oilskin pouch.

They did the same with the next, moving from canoe to canoe, while the man buying the pelts from the Cree blocked the view of anyone passing onshore. It only took a few minutes, and soon they had some eight oilskin pouches in their hands. They pulled themselves to the prow of the first canoe and up onto the shore. The oilskin pouches in their hands, they hurried away while the other men completed purchasing the pelts. Fargo swore, since he wanted to follow the two men but didn't dare while the Cree and the others were still milling about. He stayed in place until the men left carrying their pelts and the Cree climbed into their canoes and sailed away.

He swam back across the river, then pulled himself out on the protrusion of land and crouched on the ground. The night had come to cover the town, but some of the buildings had outside kerosene lamps, and the saloon cast enough light to seep across the streets. Fargo crept forward and found the wet marks on the ground where the oilskin pouches had dripped water as they were being carried away. He followed the trail and suddenly ducked behind a narrow shed as he came upon a small, sturdy hut where two rifle-toting men stood guard. The wet marks on the ground ended at the door to the hut, and as Fargo pondered getting inside the hut, the door opened and a third man emerged to take up guarding the hut. Fargo was still watching the guarded hut when he heard footsteps and the murmur of voices, and he drew back deeper into the shadows.

Four men approached and Fargo's brows lifted again as he saw that Ralph Abernoy was one of them. They halted outside the hut, and Abernoy spoke to the three guards before moving on. Fargo saw the four men enter a building only a few yards from the hut where the glow of kerosene lamps let him glimpse a table and chairs before Ralph Abernoy closed the door. Fargo's eyes returned to the hut. There was no chance of getting inside now, not with Abernoy and the other's within earshot, and he drew back and kept watch again. But Abernoy and the others stayed closeted for hours, and finally Fargo rose and in a crouch made his way to where he had left his clothes. His body had dried and he dressed quickly, strapping on the Sam Browne belt as he finished.

Some of the missing pieces were falling into place, but not enough for the final answers. Yet he knew he had to proceed with what he knew now and pursue the rest later. The Cree were still the key players. They were being used to smuggle the oilskin pouches to the town at Lanigan's Creek. At arranged places, they were met, the pouches attached to the undersides of the canoes, and they went on, six canoes of Indian trappers merely selling pelts. No one seeing them would think any differently. He sure as hell hadn't. It was those meetings, when the oilskin pouches were attached to the canoes, that the hapless victims had come upon and paid for with their lives. That much was now answered, but what did it all mean? Why were the oilskin pouches so important? Why did they have to be smuggled in? And where did Ralph Abernoy fit in?

Those remained the real questions, but there was something more important than finding the final answers. There could be no more massacres, no more innocent victims. That much had to be stopped, first, and that meant the Cree were still the core of the entire scheme. No Cree and their canoes, no smuggling. That meant reaching the canoe, first, getting to them harshly, brutally, as coldbloodedly as they had massacred the innocent victims. They'd get the message at once, Fargo knew, and he counted on something more. The Cree were realists and opportunists. They were willing to join the white man's schemes if he made it worth their while. But they wouldn't sacrifice themselves for him. Loyalty was not part of the bargain. It never was. Loyalty was reserved for blood, for tribal honor, not for the white man's little schemes.

Fargo retrieved the Ovaro and turned the horse south. Ralph Abernoy was involved, somehow, someway, perhaps more than casually, but he would have to wait, and as Fargo rode he felt the stab of excitement go through him. Caryn, he muttered, perhaps she could supply answers about Abernoy, little things that would suddenly become not at all little. He sent the pinto into a trot and moved through the night and into the aspen.

This time, when the time came for the Cree to pull ashore to rest, he only paused to watch them for a moment and then rode on. He let the Ovaro's legs take him through the forests at a steady, ground-eating pace. The moon was high and the night dark and still when he reached the Danner spread. He halted before Caryn's house and slid to the ground. He knocked softly, expecting to knock a dozen times before he woke her, and was surprised when the door opened. Caryn's eyes widened as she saw him.

"Fargo," she said, "what are you doing here?" She wore a white nightgown with a scoop neck that revealed the round fullness of her breasts.

"Came to talk," he said.

She pulled him into the house, her arms around his neck. "Not just talk. I couldn't sleep. I was thinking about you, again." She turned away, lighted a lamp on low, and its glow silhouetted the round curves of her figure through the thin material of the nightgown.

"I've things to say and answers to get," Fargo said. Caryn's eyes searched his face.

"Very serious things, I'd say," she remarked, and he nodded. She listened in silence as he told her what he'd found out. She lowered herself onto a settee when he finished.

"I'll tell you everything I know about Ralph Abernoy, but it's not that much and I don't think it'll be that important," Caryn said.

"Unimportant things can become important," Fargo said.

"But I want you to promise me something, first," Caryn said, her hands folding over his. "Don't go running off. Stay with me. I've been burning up thinking about you, wanting you. You've time. Nothing more's going to happen that quickly. Stay. Maybe I'll think of something more tomorrow. Maybe I can find a way to bring Ralph Abernoy to you."

She was making sense, Fargo thought. There'd be a

breathing space, time before another rendezvous was arranged. And she was looking absolutely gorgeous, her throbbing wanting bringing a new dimension to her. "Agreed," he said, and her lips found his at once, warmly eager, but he pulled back after a moment. "Talk, first," he grunted.

"You drive a hard bargain, Fargo," Caryn said.

"I want time to think about what you're going to tell me," he said, and Caryn sat back and pushed aside the annoyance in her clear blue eyes.

"Starting from the time I first met Ralph at my mother's," she began and proceeded to tell him what she knew about the man's habits, his businesses, often pausing to recall one thing or another. She didn't hurry what she had to say, and he listened carefully. When she finished he had nothing to tie Abernoy to the Cree or to strange, smuggled oilskin pouches. "I told you it wouldn't be that important," she said.

"It's not unimportant," Fargo said. "And maybe you'll think of something more tomorrow." She had given him a picture of a very sharp man with business dealings all over the Dominion. But then, Colonel French had told him that about Abernoy, Fargo reflected. Caryn rose, reached out to him, and he went with her as she stepped into an almost dark bedroom, only the glow of moonlight through the window affording any light. She turned to him and began to unbutton his shirt, slow, deliberate movements, not taking her eyes from his. He undid his gunbelt and let it slide to the floor, followed with trousers as she pushed his shirt from him. She stopped, her hand moving to the top of the nightgown, where she pulled a string and the garment came open to fall to the floor. He found the moonlight suddenly giving more than enough light to very round shoulders, strong and compact, in keeping with a round rib cage and breasts that were full and rounded, swaying slightly as she breathed deeply, the movement quietly provocative.

Each round, full breast was tipped by a strong, deep red nipple standing erect, a small lighter red circle around each, and his eyes went down to the compact waist, short and strong, and below it, a slightly convex little belly that also echoed the rest of her body in its fleshy fullness. Below it, reaching up with stray tendrils of black strands, a very dense triangle also beckoned, and Caryn moved and Fargo saw her thighs were full yet not without shape, her legs firm and well muscled. She moved backward with him to where a large double bed took up the front part of the room. He shed the last of his underwear as she fell onto her back and made a small pushing motion with her hips.

He came atop her and Caryn gave a long, deep sigh of satisfaction and moved under him at once, bringing one round breast up to his mouth. "Take it, take it," he heard her whisper, and he closed his lips around its firm roundness, pulling gently, feeling the erect tip against his tongue. He thought Caryn was going to be headlong in her delight as he felt her compact body move under his. But she held her own pace, her energetic body managing to push and heave and yet hold itself in, and she cried out as he rubbed back and forth across her with his mouth, his hands, and his own seeking warmth. "Oh, Jesus, that's good . . . oh, that's good," she gasped out, suddenly rolled, taking him with her. She stayed atop him as she rubbed her entire body up and down his, her fleshy legs clasping against him and small, panting sounds coming from her. When she fell back on her side he came atop her again and his fingers pushed through the very dense nap, pressing hard against the really full mound. Her hips lifted, her torso moving upward, the senses beckoning, entreating.

He found her wetness and Caryn screamed and fell back on the bed, but her hand shot down to come against his, pushing him to her. "Yes, yes, yes, yes . . . oh, God, yes," she cried, her head nodding frantically, her eyes closed, lips drawn back almost in a grimace. But it was a grimace of pleasure, he knew, and her scream was proof as he explored further. Her hands moved up and down his sides, pulling on him, urging more from him, and he let his pulsating strength push forward to touch the liquescent portal. Caryn's scream became a wild cry, and her arms came around his back, her thighs lifting to close around his buttocks, and she was pushing, bucking, exploding with all her compact strength, the body echoing the passions. He felt the power of flesh and senses, body and soul, pain and ecstasy.

But with the explosiveness that was part of her compact body, she suddenly flung arms and legs outward, away from him, and with her torso thrusting upward, she bucked and gyrated and screamed, and he could feel the wild contractions of her. He came with her, swept along by her wild passion. "Yes, Jesus, yes . . . yes, yes," Caryn Danner cried out at her climax of climaxes, and her hands pounded into the bedsheets. The turbulent, wild moment finally shattered away, and Caryn never brought her arms and legs back to embrace him. Instead, she fell backward flat, legs outspread, arms outstretched, and he lay with her, listening to the sound of her harsh breathing. Only when he moved to leave her did she wrap herself instantly around him. "Not yet," she said, holding him to her, and he lay with her until she finally sighed and moved to look at him from one elbow. "Everything I expected," she murmured.

"I admit to being surprised. You work up a mighty good head of steam," Fargo said.

"Always have. I like things my way, my speed," she said, and Fargo smiled and saw the day filtering into the room, turning it into drapes and dresser, a chair in one corner and another room adjoining. Caryn rose from the bed, her rounded, compact body still exuding energy as she pulled on a dark robe. "I'll put on the coffee kettle . . . in between," she said.

"In between?" Fargo echoed.

"Yes, I always like coffee in between," she smiled. "It makes the next round even better." She went into the next room, and Fargo rose, disdaining clothes. It seemed he'd only have to take them off again, and as he heard Caryn with the kettle, he wandered into the little nook adjoining the bedroom, his gaze taking in a square crochet table with spools of crochet wool lined up behind a pattern. But two spools were set out in the foreground, black, wider than the others, and Fargo found himself staring at them, not in idle curiosity but in recognition. They were identical to the black yarn that had been neatly wrapped around the packets of money Lisette's attackers had on them.

He felt his head spinning, a wave of shock and disbelief whirling around him. He turned as he heard Caryn's footsteps behind him, the two spools of yarn in his hand, and he realized he was pushing them at her as his eyes still sought not to believe what he held. But then his answer came, in Caryn's gaze as she saw the terrible realization forming in his stare. A tiny smile touched her eyes, almost apologetic, and she took a step sideways, reached under the crochet table, and her hand came out holding the revolver. He stared at the heavy Joslyn army revolver, a quick-firing single-action weapon. "Sorry, Fargo. I was looking forward to another fuck, honestly," she said.

Fargo felt the disbelief still clutching at him as he stared at her. "My God, it was you. You hired those killers, not Caleb Barton," he said, hardly able to believe his own words. He stared at her and saw no denial in her gaze, only a small furrow creasing her brow as she stared speculatively at him.

"If they did in Lisette how'd you know the money was wrapped in black yarn?" Caryn questioned, and he felt caution pushing through his fury.

"That's none of your damn business," he growled.

"But it is and it may be important," Caryn said.

Fargo stared at her and was angry that there was still disbelief in his voice. "You've been part of it all along. All that talk about Horace being desperate for help was a crock of shit, wasn't it? It was an attempt to keep me from tracking the Cree."

"It seemed the best move at the time," she said.

Fargo's eyes went to the Joslyn. It didn't waver. "Is Horace part of it, too?" he asked.

"No. Horace sent for you. He believes in you. Besides, he's too stupid to be involved in anything," Caryn said disdainfully.

"Where is he now?"

"On a trip," she said.

"Tonight was another move to keep me out of the way," Fargo said.

"But I did enjoy it," she said.

"Go to hell, honey," Fargo said bitterly, and again he saw that the revolver hadn't moved a fraction of an inch. His glance paused at the bedroom window, and he heard his curse, as much at himself as at her. "That Cree, I was all wrong about him. He wasn't passing by and spotting an open window. He was on his way here, to get new orders from you. You blew him away when you saw I was getting the best of him. You made sure I wouldn't get him to talk. Jesus, you're a piece of work."

"Put on the rest of your clothes," Caryn said coldly.

"Why, can't shoot somebody naked?" Fargo tossed back.

"It's easier to pull around a body with clothes on than a naked one," she said icily. "Get dressed."

He found himself looking with awe at her as he pulled on clothes and she kicked the Colt aside. He had seldom misjudged anyone as thoroughly as Caryn Danner, he realized. She waited till he had donned the scarlet jacket before motioning to him with the Joslyn. "Move. You're going to the cellar," she said.

"Getting soft-hearted? I expected a bullet," he snapped.

"You'll get one. Right now I've things to do and we have to figure the best way to get rid of you. We don't want a dead Mountie on our doorstep," Caryn Danner said. She opened a narrow door at the end of the bedroom, and he saw the flight of steps going down to the cellar. He paused to turn to her on the top step.

"You never did come here to help Horace, did you, not even when you first came. You were always part of this," he said.

"Get downstairs, *now*," Caryn hissed.

He turned, started down the steps, and he was halfway down when he felt the blow smash down on the back of his head, unmistakably the butt of the Joslyn. He felt himself falling as the world spun away to nothingness.

8

He didn't know how long he had lain unconscious; he knew only that when he woke his head hurt and he had difficulty breathing. He blinked and let the dim area come into focus and saw a square dirt and stone cellar with three heavy support beams crossing the ceiling. He quickly realized the reason for his obstructed breathing when he felt the gag over his mouth. Trying to move his arms, he saw that he couldn't. He tried his legs next with the same result and saw that he was thoroughly tied with heavy rope. In addition, his wrists and ankles were separately bound. Lifting his head, he saw that there were no windows in the cellar, the only light seeping in from under the door to the cellar and through assorted cracks.

His curses muffled by the gag, he kicked out with both his bound legs and, in a series of kicks and twists, landed thoroughly out of breath against the opposite wall. It had been an exercise in futility and frustration, he realized, and he lay still as his breath returned. The house was silent. He heard no sound from up above and wondered if he would have. Once again, for want of something to do, he kicked and rolled his way back across the floor to where the cellar stairs led from the floor above. Lying still, he listened again and heard only silence.

He tested the wrist bonds and found they were all-too securely tied. His hands behind his back, he had no way of reaching the throwing knife in his calf holster and so he decided to maneuver himself onto his back. Using his bound-together legs, he kicked upward, half propelling, half lifting himself until he got his rear onto the lowest step of the stairs. After pausing to regain his breath, he did the same thing and managed to get his rear onto the second step. With the excitement of hope pushing through him, he kicked and lifted again and brought his rear onto the third step. He was close to standing on his head from the steep incline of the steps but, excitement surging through him, he kicked out again, flung his body upward with the kick, and landed on the fourth step. But only for an instant, as gravity and balance took over and he felt himself toppling over and backward. He winced as he fell down the steps and realized he could have broken his neck as he lay on the cellar floor on his stomach.

The gag muffled his curses as he finally turned himself over and came to rest against the wall near the foot of the stairs. He lay there, helpless with rage and frustration, wracking his mind for a way out and finding none. He closed his eyes and rested, bitterly aware that he had not a damn thing else to do. He knew, in a vague way, that the hours were passing, but he had no way of knowing how many had gone by. The cellar had become a small tomb that sealed away all sense of time, almost of place. Lying awake, with his eyes closed, he suddenly heard a sound and he snapped to attention, his ears straining to catch it again. He was beginning to think he had imagined the sound when it came again, this time from almost directly above him, and it took form as the creak of a floorboard.

He frantically spun his body around and began to kick against the wall with both feet, pounding the wall as hard as his bound legs would permit him to do. It seemed to take hours, but he knew it was only minutes when he heard the cellar door open and the sound of footsteps descending. He turned his head, saw the bottom of the fringed deerskin skirt, then the top of it, and then the short, leather vest. He stared at the rest of the slender lithe figure as it appeared, his eyes wide over the top of the gag, and he saw the rifle in her hands. Lisette rested the rifle against the wall and first took the gag from his mouth.

"My God, you," Fargo gasped, blurting the words out in a rush of breath. "I don't understand. What are you doing here?"

"I came looking for you," she said as she began to untie his wrist ropes, first, then the heavier ropes around his body.

"How come? How'd you come to be here?" Fargo asked as, his hands freed, he began to untie the ankle bonds. "You were with Colonel French," he said.

"I never did get there," Lisette said, her handsome face expressionless.

He stared at her, the frown deepening as a sudden flood of realization swept over him. "You," he gasped out. "You were the one in the hills. You were watching me all along."

She offered a half shrug. "Not all along," she said as he pushed to his feet. "I watched the Cree downriver while you took off upriver, and sometimes I watched them on my own. But I found you when you came back.

I roamed some, watched you, watched the Cree. I stayed back. I was careful. I knew how easily you could pick up on me."

"You did a good job of being careful," Fargo said with grudging admiration. "But how'd you know I was here?"

"I didn't, not at first," Lisette said as she led the way up the stairs. "But I couldn't find you anywhere. You didn't come back with the Cree and I started looking for you. I wound up here. There was nobody around."

"Then what made you think I was here?"

"Somebody made a mistake. They left the Ovaro outside," she said. "Now suppose you tell me why you were all tied up in the cellar."

He began with discovering the oilskin pouches and finished with finding the black yarn. He omitted Caryn's passions, but he told of her admissions. Lisette blew a deep breath of surprise when he ended the recounting. "Now what? We go after Ralph Abernoy and the oilskin pouches? And little Caryn Danner, too, I'd guess," she said.

"No, the Cree, first. Caryn passed on orders. I'm betting they're going to pick up another set of the pouches," Fargo said.

"And massacre anybody who happens to be in the wrong place," Lisette said.

"Exactly. We're going to send them a message, first. They'll know what it means," Fargo said.

"You think that they'll be quick to get out of the smuggling business," Lisette said.

"For two reasons. One, they'll realize the price is suddenly too high, and two, they won't have anything to smuggle when we take care of Abernoy and little Caryn."

She nodded as they rode from the Danner place and into the hills, but he saw the sideways glance she tossed at him, and she allowed a small shrug. "You stop to think that neither of those things are going to be easy?" she remarked.

"I know they're not going to be easy," Fargo said. "What else are you saying?"

"Maybe we should go back to Colonel French and get some help," she said.

"No," he said. "More innocent people could be killed while we're doing that and we'd give Abernoy a chance to get rid of the pouches and cover his tracks. Once Caryn comes back and finds I'm gone she'll know they'll have to shift their own plans."

Lisette nodded again and rode beside him as he led the way into the hills to halt within sight of the Cree camp. Their canoes were pulled onto the shore, and Fargo allowed a bitter smile. It was all he needed to see to know they were still waiting. As the day began to fade, he found an alcove of white spruce a few hundred feet higher and put down his bedroll. Lisette ate some of the dried beef strips with him as night fell and the half-moon rose. The meal finished, he stretched out, and she came to rest beside him, propped up on one elbow, and she let one finger idly trace a pattern on his shirt.

"I'm glad for one thing," she said.

"What's that?"

"I never knew how vicious Caryn Danner was until you told me what she'd done. But I told you she had eyes for you, and I still say I was right about that. But all this got in the way. She never got the chance to enjoy you, and I'm glad for that," Lisette said.

"I am, too," Fargo said blandly. After all, he muttered silently, it wasn't as though he'd sought out Caryn Danner. In fact, he had been used, he told himself, grateful for the powers of rationalization. Lisette's hand opened the vest and shrugged it aside and he took in the lovely shallow curve of her breasts, the flat deep pink nipples, and he eagerly seized the lovely gift that pushed aside conscience. He leaned over, drew first one breast into his mouth, then moved to the other, and in moments they were entwined, flesh to flesh, desire to desire, and he reveled in the soft, sensuous movements of her lithe slenderness.

Lisette wrapped herself around him, but in her wanting there was sweetness, in her strength there was softness. She stroked him with her legs, her hands, her breasts, low, deep moanings coming from the very core of her until her cries, smothered against his chest, echoed the ecstasy of that exploding moment. She lay beside him, finally, breasts against his chest, flat, virginal-like points pressed hard to him, and in her sigh of contentment he knew he would never understand the mysteries of woman. Nor would any man, he told himself, not now, not ever, for they were the keepers of the real secret of love, and only they would know its full dimensions.

He slept with her, content to know no more, and when the day broke he woke first, found a small stream in which to wash, and dried and dressed, enjoyed Lisette's lithe body as she used the stream. Finally, he walked her horse beside his as he moved down closer to the Cree camp, and he felt the tension grip him at once as he saw six of the canoes being loaded with pelts. "They're getting ready to move," he murmured. "Only we're going to move ahead of them." She swung onto her horse and rode beside him as he sent the Ovaro forward through the tree cover. "You've your rifle and I've my Henry.

133

That little bitch has my Colt with her so we'll have to do it all with the rifles." He rode on perhaps a half a mile before turning down to the water, went on another few thousand feet, and his face wrinkled into a grimace. "Up there . . . half mile, maybe," he said.

Lisette followed his gaze and saw the spring wagon, outfitted with a fringed top, four women riding inside it. "They don't know how lucky they are," she murmured as Fargo drew to a halt, turned the Ovaro into a line of sandbar willows, and dismounted. He drew the big Henry from its saddle case and knelt on one knee as Lisette settled herself a dozen feet from him. "I'll start with the Cree, you take the canoes. When you're finished with the canoes, you can finish the Cree. Don't show them any mercy. They don't deserve it."

Lisette nodded and took another grip on her rifle as Fargo's eyes peered downriver. The six canoes took almost a half hour to appear, but finally they paddled into sight, three Cree in each canoe as they had all the other times. Fargo waited, let them near, and saw the Indians in the lead canoe gesticulate to the others. They had caught sight of the distant spring wagon and immediately started to paddle faster. The lead canoe was almost abreast of where Fargo and Lisette crouched in the willows. "Ladies first," he said, and Lisette began firing. She raked the line of canoes with gunfire, and the water spurted into them like so many tiny fountains. The Cree, completely taken by surprise at first, took almost a minute of confusion to recover. It was a fatal minute as Fargo sent a raking volley from the big, fast-firing Henry.

The three Cree in the first canoe went down, two draped over the sides of their canoe. Two more in the next boat spun in a grotesque dance as they toppled into the water. He had swung the rifle in a wide sweep and saw two of the Cree in the last canoe fall to the bottom of the boat as the water already began to send it sinking to the bottom of the river. Some of the Cree dove into the water and swam for the opposite bank, but he saw Lisette's shots end their swim. A quick count showed him that six of the Indians made it to the opposite bank, half running and the rest crawling to the edge of the trees. Fargo had reloaded and took down one more before he made it to the tree cover. All six canoes were filled with water, two of them sinking out of sight as he watched.

Fargo glimpsed the remaining Cree running away, staying inside the trees as they fled. "They'll make their way back to camp," he heard Lisette say.

"Where they'll spread the word that the white man's scheme has blown up," Fargo said. He rose, put the rifle in its case, and swung onto the Ovaro, and Lisette rode with him as he headed upriver along the bank. Around a slow curve, the spring wagon came into sight with the four women inside it, but Fargo's eyes caught the movement in the stand of aspen a few yards ahead of the wagon. "Shit," he swore as he sent the Ovaro forward. "Get your rifle," he threw back at Lisette, and she pulled the gun from its case just as the riders raced from the trees. Three white men and four Cree, Fargo saw, racing for the wagon. He had the big Henry in his hands as he saw the women turn in surprise as the horsemen charged toward them. His first shots took down two of the Cree and he heard Lisette fire. A third Cree fell to the ground and the fourth pulled his pony around. The three white man had reined up, and one ducked as Fargo's shot grazed his head.

The man shouted and the others turned instantly, racing away into the trees. Lisette fired, and Fargo saw the fourth Cree kick at his pony as a red crease appeared on his shoulder. Fargo slowed and met Lisette's questioning frown. "No, they're going to keep running," he said. "No point in chasing after them. Their rendezvous is over and we've better things to do." She put her rifle away as he pushed his into its case and moved forward to where the four women in the wagon waited, relief pushing aside the fright in their faces.

"Thank you," the one said. "Thank you both. Who were they? Why'd they come after us?"

"It's a long story, ladies," Fargo said. "Let's just say they were going to add you to the list of poor souls who were in the wrong place at the wrong time. Go your way and say an extra prayer for yourselves tonight."

"We'll do that, and another for the both of you," the woman called after Fargo and Lisette as they rode on. She rode without questions as he followed the river till night came and then slept happily beside him. When morning came, her eyes questioned when he turned north to Lanigan's Creek.

"Another few hours. We'll get there by dark," he told her.

"Where, exactly?"

"A hut in a little town. They're keeping the oilskin pouches inside it and I want to know what's in those pouches important enough to enlist the Cree as smugglers and killers," Fargo said.

"Caryn's probably discovered that you got away by

now. Won't she be on her way to tell Abernoy?" Lisette queried.

"Maybe. I'd guess so. And Abernoy has some associates in whatever this is. They could be there with him," Fargo said. "If Caryn stayed back waiting for him, he might not know I'm on the loose. I've got to be ready for it to go either way. That's where you come in." Lisette's brows lifted in question. "Nobody knows you're alive. I want to keep it that way a little longer."

"Explain."

"I'm going in. You stay back out of sight, someplace where you can see what's going on. I'll find a spot for you. If you see things go wrong you step in. You'll be my ace in the hole. Again," he added, and he caught her little smile. He kept a steady pace and reached the stretch of open land just as dark began to roll over the protrusion of land the canoes had used to bring their journey to an end. By the time he passed the spot, the darkness had settled in, and he slowed and nodded to the houses beyond the shoreline. He walked the Ovaro through a narrow space between two houses and came in sight of the hut and beyond it, the building he'd seen Abernoy enter with his friends. Only a single guard stood in front of the hut. "Good," Fargo grunted, and Lisette frowned back. "That means they're not expecting me," he explained as he dismounted.

"I'll stay here," Lisette said. "I've a good view from here and I'm in deep shadows."

Fargo nodded in agreement as a quick glance around showed him no better spot. The nearby buildings were all dark, only the saloon showing a circle of light in the distance. "You hang in here unless you see things go wrong. I might be back with all the answers we want,"

Fargo said and slid from the saddle. He thought about taking the rifle with him and decided against it. Bending down, he drew the thin blade from his calf holster and slipped it up his sleeve, the hilt resting in his palm. Lisette's hand brushed his face as he stepped from the narrow space between the buildings and turned to cross in front of the hut. He walked slowly, casually, and saw the guard stiffen at once when he came closer.

"That's far enough, mister," the man said.

"Just passin' by," Fargo said and took two steps closer.

"Keep walking," the guard said, and Fargo shuffled on until he was opposite the man.

"Got a light?" he asked. "I got the cigar but I need a light. I need a smoke real bad." He edged closer to the guard, moving on short, shuffling steps and saw the man reach into his pocket with one hand as he cradled the rifle across his chest. Fargo slid another step closer to the guard as the man brought out a lucifer and started to hand it to him. With the speed of a puma's strike, Fargo's arm shot out, the knife dropping into his palm and the guard's eyes widened as he felt the tip of the narrow blade against his throat. "No noise or this'll come out your ear," Fargo hissed. "Turn around." The man obeyed, and Fargo's left arm whipped around the man's neck and tightened. His right hand came around, pressed into the underside of the man's jaw, and in seconds the man slid unconscious to the ground.

Fargo picked up the rifle as he dragged the man to the door of the hut and tried the knob. Only slightly surprised that the door opened, Fargo saw the kerosene lamp on the floor just inside the door. Leaving the door open just enough for him to see, he lighted the lamp and quickly pulled the guard inside and rolled him into a corner. He'd be unconscious long enough, Fargo knew, and he lifted his eyes to the room and found two long tables covered with the oilskin pouches. He began to open the pouches in the first row, then those in the second, until he had emptied all the pouches of the first table. He found himself staring at the material spread out in front of him, surprise wrestling with incomprehension as he stared at an array of documents, official government documents, all bearing the seal of the Dominion of Canada, with some carrying provincial stamps.

He took in land deeds, property assignment forms, court orders with blank spaces to be filled in, town charter forms, prisoner release forms, again with blank spaces to be properly completed, government bank drafts with amounts up to two thousand dollars per draft, mining claim forms, waterway rights documents, and boxes on boxes of election ballots with candidates' names to be filled in. Fargo was still frowning as he went to the second table. He hadn't known what to expect to find inside the pouches, but he certainly hadn't expected this. Opening the pouches on the second table, he spilled out pouch after pouch of Canadian paper currency, the bills ranging in amounts from ten dollars Canadian to a hundred dollars each.

He was staring at the money and the array of documents, wondering what it all meant, when the door flew open. He tried to reach the rifle, but stopped midway as he saw Caryn, his Colt in her hand, and Ralph Abernoy beside her holding a Remington six-shot single-action army revolver. Abernoy pushed the door closed behind as they stepped into the hut, and Fargo saw the surprise in her eyes as she spoke to Abernoy without taking her eyes from him. "You were right," she murmured.

"Of course," Abernoy said, a faint smile on his face.

"How did you get loose back at the house?" Caryn asked Fargo, her eyes cold.

"Horace came back and found me. I told him to get away from there," Fargo said, and he saw the uncertainty in Caryn's eyes as, unwilling to simply accept his answer, she was aware that it was entirely plausible.

"We left only one guard here," Abernoy broke in. "We knew you'd see that as proof everything was still here. We stayed back behind the other buildings and looked in every fifteen minutes. When the guard wasn't there we knew you were."

Fargo nodded unhappily. He had walked into their trap, his haste overcoming his normal caution, and his eyes returned to the documents and currency on the tables. "I made a mistake," he admitted. "And I'll be damned if I understand any of this, except for the money. I can understand smuggling money."

Abernoy's smile was made of smug confidence. "Only the documents are even more important," he said, and Fargo's eyes questioned. "I don't mind telling you what they all mean, seeing as how you won't be passing it any further. All those documents are forgeries."

"Forgeries?" Fargo echoed in surprise.

"Completely. You see, the Dominion government has agents all over, especially around Regina and Winnipeg. They know there are numerous groups unfriendly to the proposed federation. We couldn't risk one of those agents coming onto these documents. Our entire plan would blow up, so we had to find a way to get them past these agents to here, where we'll be shipping them further north for storage."

"And the money?" Fargo questioned.

"Counterfeit," Abernoy said.

Fargo frowned at the man. "Forged documents and counterfeit money you're sending north to store away. I don't get it. Why send it away? What the hell does it mean?"

"I think you've said enough, Ralph," Caryn put in.

"Nonsense, my dear. I'm enjoying his confusion. It speaks well for our plans," Abernoy said. "I'll tell him the rest and enjoy watching his grudging admiration." The man moved closer to the tables as he left Caryn to keep the Colt aimed at Fargo. He ran his hands almost lovingly over the table of documents. "Very soon the new government will finish acquiring all the Hudson Bay Company land. That will set the signal for the new central Dominion government. They'll bring all their bureaucratic rules and regulations. That Mountie uniform you're wearing is just one small example of what they'll be trying to do, perhaps a particularly stupid example."

"And you don't want any of that," Fargo said.

"That's right. My associates and I intend to do everything we can to show that this Dominion Federation won't work. When the Crown finally realizes this new Dominion is not working, that it's nothing but chaos, they'll withdraw support for it, and Robertson Ross, Butler, and John MacDonald will go down with it."

"And you'll be there, owning and controlling big pieces of Canada to do with whatever you like, and they'll have to deal with you," Fargo said.

"Precisely," Abernoy said. "All these documents and all this counterfeit money are going to be used to sew chaos. We'll create so many tangles and conflicts, so much confusion and dissension the Dominion will fall apart from outside and inside."

Fargo allowed a grim snort, not of admiration but of realization. Their scheme was entirely possible. They had planned carefully and well, and his eyes moved across the array of forged documents. There were more than enough to sew chaos in even an established government. A new one would certainly be brought down. He was still pondering the ugly truth of it when the door opened, and he saw Lisette step into the room, rifle in hand and aimed.

"Drop your guns," she said as Caryn and Abernoy turned. Both hesitated a moment, but Lisette stepped into the hut and moved to one side so that both Caryn and Abernoy were in a line with the rifle. "I'm going to get two for the price of one," Lisette said, and Caryn lowered the Colt, letting it slide from her fingers to the floor. Abernoy took the Remington from his belt and dropped it on the floor.

"Two can play at hanging back," Fargo said as he stepped forward. He moved past Caryn and bent down to pick up the Colt. Her foot, only six inches from him, lashed out in a lightninglike sideways kick, and the blow caught him alongside the temple. He heard his gasp of sharp pain, and then Caryn was atop him, clawing at his eyes as he fell forward, rolling with him. Lisette's shot went wild, and she held back, unable to get another clear shot. Out of the corner of his eyes, Fargo saw Abernoy try for his gun, but Lisette fired again and he rolled away. Caryn's fingernails digging into his closed eyes, Fargo flung himself sideways as he dug an elbow into her ribs. She gave a gasp of breath, but she clung to him as a leaf clings to a rock, and her leg kicked out. Fargo heard the shattering of glass and the instant roar of flame, and Caryn's grip fell away as she, too, turned to see the kerosene lamp shooting flame. The paper documents caught at once, the flame hungrily devouring the nearest ones who immediately leaped to the next nearest.

"No, Jesus, no," Fargo heard Abernoy scream. The man raced across the room, trying to gather up documents and counterfeit money and fling them away from harm. But the fire had leapt into an instant pillar of flame that sprang, not unlike a hungry animal, to the walls of the hut, instantly devouring. Fargo felt the heat of it as a leaping tongue roared up alongside him, and he had to fling himself away. He turned to see Lisette, the rifle in her hands, holding Caryn, where she lay on the floor.

"Get out, crawl out," Lisette said, but suddenly the wall alongside her erupted in a sheet of fire, and Lisette dropped halfway down as she twisted away. Caryn kicked out with both feet, catching Lisette in the back, and Fargo saw the rifle fly from Lisette's hands as she went down. The gun fell into the flaming wall, and a succession of shots joined the roar of fire. Fargo made a grab for Caryn as she dived past him. He missed, and he saw her go rolling out the door. He swung his body around and got one hand on Lisette's arm as she had to fling herself sideways to avoid another leaping wall of flame. He yanked, half pulling and half throwing her out the door to safety, and then spun to see Abernoy. The man was in the far corner of the hut where the flames hadn't reached yet. He was stuffing documents and money into the oilskin pouches, shouting protests and curses, a man who had snapped as he saw all his plans vanishing in flame.

Ducking low, Fargo dove past a sideways flare of fire, reached Abernoy, and he seized the man by one arm. "Get out, you damn fool. Another minute and this place is going to be all flames," he said.

"No, no," Abernoy yelled, pulling away from him, a man crazed and obsessed. Fargo glanced at the flames that were consuming the hut and everything in it, and he wondered who was maddest, he or Abernoy. He lunged after Abernoy again as he felt the flames against his face, pulled the man back, and crossed a short right to his jaw. He caught Abernoy as the man started to go down and flung him over one shoulder. The flames seared now, reaching out at him with fiery fingers as he ran, carrying Abernoy. He glimpsed the doorway through a moment's break in the curtain of flame and half leapt, half dived, and felt himself hit the doorstep and tumble out into the night, Abernoy rolling away. Fargo regained his feet and took a moment to see the hut consumed in fire, the flames soaring upward, the rear wall collapsing in a shower of burning embers.

He cursed as he realized that his Colt was inside the flaming structure, and he glanced up the street now glowing from the fire. "Lisette," he called, but there was no answer, and he ran to where she'd left her horse. The short-legged brown gelding was gone, and he cursed as he knew that Caryn's horse would be gone, also. He turned as Abernoy regained his consciousness and started to push to his feet. Fargo had hold of the man, shaking him as though he were a rag doll. "She's got Lisette. Somehow, she got hold of Lisette. Where'd she go?"

"How do I know?" the man said.

Fargo drove a hard right into Abernoy's stomach, and the man dropped to his knees. "Because she didn't just run. She's headed someplace and you know where," Fargo said. "I'll throw you into the goddamn fire if you don't talk."

"I don't know," Abernoy gasped, and Fargo seized him by the back of his shirt and his trousers, lifted, and, as though he were swinging a sack of potatoes, started to throw Abernoy into the blazing hut. "No . . . Jesus, no," Abernoy screamed. "All right, all right." Fargo half turned midway through his throw, and Abernoy landed alongside the blazing hut, where he frantically rolled away from a tongue of flames that licked out at him. Pouncing on him at once, Fargo yanked the man to his feet. "Talk, goddamn you," he rasped.

"There's a house, north, at Carrot River. It's where we were going to store everything. She's probably heading there," Abernoy said.

"Get your horse," Fargo ordered as he pulled Abernoy to his feet and sent him stumbling toward the big bay stallion as he ran to the Ovaro and leapt onto the saddle. "Ride!" Fargo shouted and set off with Abernoy as the man turned north and followed Lanigan's Creek. Abernoy's bay stallion was a strong horse, and Fargo set a furious pace as he rode with the terrible unknown hanging around his neck. Did Caryn want a hostage or was she simply fleeing? Did she still have Lisette with her or had she killed her by now? How did she manage to get the better of Lisette? The questions pounded inside him, each one holding an answer to the others, and he swore into the night wind as he rode beside Abernoy.

The man turned slightly east as they left Lanigan's

Creek behind, and Fargo saw they rode through land that was open and studded with clusters of balsam poplar and paper birch. Sharply etched ridges parallel to each other, he saw with the last of the moon as it slid toward the horizon. Abernoy knew better than to try and slow his pace, yet the ride seemed endless, and Fargo felt his spirits dropping with each mile. "If she's dead, you're dead," he said to Abernoy.

"That's not fair. I can't control what she's doing," the man protested.

"You called the shots. You pay the price," Fargo flung back as he saw the end of the night turn to the first streaks of dawn. "How much further?" he rasped.

"Not far," Abernoy said, and Fargo felt the Ovaro slowing and saw Abernoy's stallion dropping back further. He pulled the Ovaro in, unwilling to let Abernoy ride behind him. But it had been a headlong pace, and Fargo knew they should have caught up to Caryn. His eyes scanned the land ahead as it took shape in the spreading daylight, and suddenly he glimpsed the two horses on a ridge almost opposite from where he and Abernoy rode. He reined the Ovaro in at once and Abernoy stopped with him. Caryn rode a half pace behind Lisette atop the flat ridge, and he saw Lisette was the first to see him. Caryn turned then, peered across at him, and Fargo saw her draw the small pistol from inside her shirt.

"Keeping riding or you're dead, bitch," he heard Caryn scream to Lisette, who spurred the gelding on. But the horse had little strength left to respond as Caryn drove upward toward the top of the ridge. One side of the ridge became a steep cliff at the top, he saw, the other side a steep slope that led down to a thin line of blue water and a square house near the shore. He cast a glance at Abernoy, who sat quietly on his hard-breathing stallion, his eyes nervously flicking to Fargo.

"Sit your horse," Fargo growled. "Try anything and I'll kill you." Abernoy made no reply, but Fargo saw a glint of triumph creeping into the man's eyes. Fargo's glance went back to the opposite ridge and his lips drew back in despair. It would take him at least two minutes, maybe three, to make the ride down the slope and up the other incline to reach the far ridge. Caryn would be at the top of the ridge long before, he knew, and she had the only gun. He pondered making the run, anyway, a desperate race that might unsettle her. But before he could send the Ovaro down the slope, Caryn turned in the saddle and fired a single shot, and Fargo had to fling himself sideways from the saddle as the bullet almost took his head off. The shot had been to kill or to dissuade, and as he pushed to one knee he saw Caryn charging to the top of the ridge behind Lisette.

He heard the sound of Abernoy's stallion being spun, and he rose to his feet as the man started to charge away down the ridge. Using every muscle in his powerful legs, Fargo raced at an angle toward the stallion, leapt into the air, and flung himself into the side of the horse. He got one arm around Abernoy's leg, clung to it, and Abernoy came out of the saddle to land with him in a clump of brush. Abernoy tried to wrestle free, but Fargo was on him, flinging him to the side where, as Abernoy tried to charge, the looping right landed flush on the point of his jaw, and Abernoy went down and lay still.

Fargo turned to peer across at the opposite ridge. Caryn had halted, her eyes watching the short battle for a moment, and Fargo saw Lisette seize that moment to kick out with one leg. Her blow landed in the small of Caryn's back and the compact woman flew from the saddle to land facedown on the ground, the gun flying from her hand. Lisette was already out of the saddle, racing toward the gun as Caryn dove forward to get it. She had her fingers closed around the butt when Lisette's kick sent it out of her grip again. This time the pistol skidded over the edge of the cliff, where it bounced noisily down the rocks, firing off one shot as it did.

Fargo rose to see Caryn's powerful form charge into Lisette in a flying tackle. Lisette went down and Fargo watched Caryn use her compact strength to half smother the taller girl, holding her down and bringing a forearm around to press into Lisette's throat. Lisette tried to get away, but she was thoroughly pinned, and Fargo could see the color draining from her face as Caryn's forearm choked the breath from her. "Goddamn, goddamn," he swore bitterly when he saw both of Lisette's long arms lift up, her fingers sinking into Caryn's almost-blond hair, and suddenly Caryn Danner was screaming in pain as her head was pulled to one side. Lisette twisted out from under Caryn's weight as the compact form lifted, kicked out as she did, and caught Caryn in the ribs. Pushing to her feet, Lisette turned in time to see Caryn coming at her again, but this time Caryn didn't charge. Instead, she came in with short, strong arms punching and clawing, and Fargo saw Lisette give ground.

"Look out, dammit," Fargo screamed as Lisette's feet came close to the edge of the cliff behind her, and he saw her manage to dance away. But Caryn stayed after her, in a half crouch, as Lisette danced away again. Fargo cast a quick glance at Abernoy. He was still unconscious and his horse had halted a few yards away, glad to stop running. His eyes on the two women again, Fargo saw Lisette twist away from Caryn's sweeping blows, and then, on her long, lithe legs, she feinted, feinted again, and sank a straight punch past Caryn's up-raised arms. It struck the young woman hard in the abdomen, and Caryn fell backward, half bent over. Lisette's long arms let her rake Caryn's face with a sweeping blow, and long red lines dripped from Caryn's cheek as she twisted away.

With a scream of rage and pain, Caryn flew at her foe, head lowered and blood spattering through the air. Lisette braced herself to meet the charge as Fargo shouted at her. "No, dammit, no," he cried out, but Lisette held her ground, striking out with both hands, and Fargo saw the blood suddenly come from Caryn's nose. But she had miscalculated the strength still in Caryn's compact body. She staggered backward as Caryn slammed into her, then went down as Caryn bulled forward instantly. This time Lisette rolled and tried to twist away, but Caryn was too quick, falling on her from behind, wrapping one arm around Lisette's neck. Fargo cursed in helplessness as he saw Caryn's arm tightening, twisting, turning Lisette's neck. Lisette's hands rose and flailed at the shorter form atop her, but Caryn kept her grip, slowly twisting.

Fargo felt his fists pounding into the ground as he saw Lisette's face turning red, and then he saw Lisette manage to bring one long, lithe leg up under and dig her heel into the ground. She pushed with the last of her strength and Fargo saw Caryn's form being lifted into the air. Using a last burst of breath, Lisette executed a back flip and Caryn lost her grip as she landed on her back. Lisette flung herself aside, rolled, and regained her feet as Caryn charged again. Again, Fargo shouted and Lisette glanced over her shoulder to see the edge of the cliff only inches behind her.

But Caryn Danner was charging, diving with arms outstretched. With no time to turn away and no space to maneuver, Lisette dropped to her hands and knees. Caryn's compact body landed across the top of her head and on her back, and Lisette, again making use of the leverage afforded by her long legs, threw herself upward. She felt Caryn go up and over her back in a somersault without control. Caryn's scream came, a piercing shriek, and Lisette turned her head in time to see Caryn Danner disappear over the edge of the cliff. The scream continued, a terrible sound that grew higher and thinner until it ended with blood-curdling abruptness.

Fargo rose and saw Lisette lying facedown on the ridge, her fingers digging into the ground, and he could see her shoulders shaking with sobs. Survival was often more a thing of relief than victory, he knew. He looked across at Abernoy and saw him standing, staring down at the rocks at the bottom of the cliff. Finally, he turned away and met Fargo's eyes. His shrug was defensive. "She wanted in," he muttered.

"And you were happy to use her," Fargo said. "One more reason to hang you."

He glanced to the ridge to see Lisette on her feet, pulling herself onto the brown gelding. She nosed the horse down to where she could cross the dip of land to where he waited, and when she reached him she slid down into his arms, clinging to him. "It all happened so fast," she murmured. "When I fell out of that hut with her, she pulled the gun from inside her shirt. She'd have killed me there if I hadn't gone with her. I decided to try to buy some time. I didn't know if you'd get out of the hut. I just kept hoping you had."

"Mount up," Fargo said, pressing her arm gently. "We've riding to do." He turned to Abernoy, the man's handsome face now bearing a new sullenness. "I don't want any trouble out of you," Fargo said to him as he took the lariat from the Ovaro's saddle and first bound Abernoy's wrists together in front of him so he could hold on to the saddle horn of his horse. He tied another length of lariat around the man's waist and wrapped the other end around the horn of the Ovaro's saddle.

"This isn't necessary," Abernoy complained.

"I don't aim to take any chances, seeing as how we don't have any guns," Fargo said.

"Can we buy a gun someplace?" Lisette asked. "I've some money with me."

"So do I. Maybe we can pick one up in Regina. I'll replace my Colt at a gunsmith I know back home," Fargo said as he swung onto the Ovaro and led the way south, Lisette beside him, Abernoy riding a dozen feet away. The day began to draw to a close when they neared the cluster of buildings at Lanigan's Creek, and Fargo steered the horses in a wide circle away from the town. "Mr. Abernoy has associates who were involved in this with him. They may be in town and I wouldn't want them catching sight of their partner. I'm sure they'd be quick to try and set him loose," Fargo said with a quick glance at Abernoy. The man's face remained sullen. "Maybe you'd like to give me their names," Fargo suggested.

"Go to hell," Abernoy muttered.

"I'll put it another way. A little cooperation might persuade Colonel French not to hang you," Fargo said.

"Nobody's going to hang me. I've connections in high places," Abernoy said.

Fargo's mouth became a thin line. He knew the man was not simply bragging. All the concrete evidence of his scheme had gone up in flames, and the Cree certainly weren't going to come forward and say they were involved in massacre and smuggling. His connections in high places might just enable him to wriggle free, Fargo realized, and he cursed silently. He continued the long circle around the town, and it was night when he came back to the shore of Lanigan's Creek. He found a spot in the trees back from the shoreline to bed down, used another length of lariat to tie Abernoy securely to one of the trees, and then lay down with Lisette and let exhaustion wrap both of them together.

When morning came, he led the way south again, bordered the river, and it was midafternoon when they neared the tributary that bypassed Regina. He halted, his gaze focused in the distance, and Lisette read the questions in his thoughts. "You're wondering about trying to buy a gun in Regina," she said, and he nodded.

"I'm wondering if some of his friends might be in Regina," Fargo said. "It's too damn possible, especially if they know what happened to the hut by now."

"Yes, Regina's a place they'd probably go to meet," Lisette agreed.

"I'm not going to risk it. We'll take our chances without guns and get to Colonel French," Fargo said as he sent the Ovaro forward.

He followed the tributary bypass and turned west along the river, riding beside the bank to save time going through the thick tree cover. He had gone perhaps another three miles, he guessed, when he saw three canoes appear from around a curve, four Cree in each. They slowed and turned toward him, and Fargo felt the apprehension curl through him. When the line of Cree on horseback silently filed out of the trees, he drew to a halt, his apprehension now grim fear. The Cree on horseback faced him as the three canoes came to a halt against the bank.

He cast a glance at Abernoy. "They've come to set me free," the man said, but Fargo saw the frown of uncertainty that clouded Abernoy's face. The man's eyes darted back and forth, and he was clearly uneasy.

"You think so?" Lisette asked Fargo.

Fargo pondered for a moment. "No," he said.

"Why don't you think so?" Lisette questioned.

"I think they would've come charging," Fargo said.

"They're just taking their time. They always do," Abernoy cut in, but Fargo heard the nervousness in his voice.

"You don't believe him," Lisette said to Fargo.

"No, and he doesn't believe himself," Fargo answered.

"Then what?" Lisette asked.

"I don't know," he murmured. "But I'm going to play my own game." She frowned back. "I'm going to make sure they know what I'm doing. You fall back some," he told her and pulled Abernoy toward him with the lariat until the man was positioned directly behind him. Giving himself the full length of the rope, which put Abernoy some ten feet behind him, Fargo walked the Ovaro forward. He pushed out his chest and sat very straight in the saddle so the scarlet jacket caught the full light of the sun. He was letting the picture talk, the scene make a statement that said he was an officer of the Northwest

Mounted Police, bringing in his prisoner. He was bringing in a man defeated, a man no longer powerful.

He was also challenging them to defy his authority, now an authority of victory. It was a bold move, he realized all too well, but then he had no other moves to make. And he desperately tried to invoke one more factor. The Cree were not unaware that the face of Canada was changing. They would be cautious, unwilling to open themselves for more trouble than they needed to take on. He was hoping, he knew, and all too aware that where Indians were concerned, predictions of behavior were always gambles. But he kept the Ovaro at a steady walk and cast another glance back at Abernoy. Little beads of perspiration stood out on the man's forehead. Fargo uttered a grim snort. The trickle of perspiration ran down his back under the scarlet jacket.

The movement caught his ears, almost soft, and he flashed a glance at the Cree. Almost as one, they had raised their bows, arrows in place, and he saw the bowstrings quiver as they released. His eyes snapped shut for an involuntary moment, a reaction to knowing there was no time to run and no place to run to. When he forced his eyes open, the pull came against his arm, but he felt no arrowheads piercing his body. He glanced behind him. Ralph Abernoy lay on the ground, looking not unlike a grotesque pin cushion, at least two dozen arrows in him.

Fargo shot a glance at Lisette, who simply stared down at Abernoy, her face drained of color, and Fargo's eyes went to the Cree. The horsemen were already fading back into the trees, those in the canoes already paddling downstream. Fargo felt the long breath of relief escape his lips as he leaned down and cut the lariat around Abernoy. His eyes lingered on the man for a moment. "You were right. Nobody's going to hang you," he said. He straightened in the saddle and motioned for Lisette to come alongside him. He rode off with her and saw her eyes on him.

"Why?" she asked.

"When we hit them the other day they knew things had gone sour, but they weren't that sure. They came looking and found us. Abernoy was my prisoner," Fargo said.

"You made sure they knew that."

"Right. That finished him. He was no more good to them, and they knew it. He was only a liability, and he had the power to accuse them in detail. They took care of that and avoided a head-on clash with the law, a coup and a gesture."

"You're saying they're offering no more massacres," Lisette remarked.

"Something like that. With Abernoy's scheme gone they'll simmer down. Until something else comes along and that's the best of it for now," Fargo said. He put the pinto into a trot. "Let's move. We've a report to give Colonel French."

They reached Moose Jaw soon after midday and met with the colonel in his office. When Fargo finished, French allowed a low whistle of admiration. "Splendid, splendid indeed, more than I dared hope for, Fargo," he said. "Sure you wouldn't like to become a Canadian citizen and stay on as one of my Mounties?"

"Thanks for the offer," Fargo smiled, and the colonel knew the meaning in the reply.

"I've a man arriving next week to take your place," Colonel French said.

"He'll have plenty of work waiting for him," Fargo said.

"I'll tell him how you got your man and let him know I'll expect no less from him," Colonel French said and paused in thought. "I want it to become known everywhere that the Mounties always get their man."

"Not a bad slogan," Fargo said.

"No, not at all. I'll make it ours," the colonel said.

"I'll be getting into my clothes, now," Fargo said.

"They're waiting for you in the closet," French said, and as Fargo changed out of the uniform and hung the scarlet jacket on a wall peg, he heard the colonel and Lisette talking softly in the adjoining room. When he returned to the office, the colonel offered a small shrug. "Lisette's agreed to stay on to help my new man," he said. "As soon as she gets back."

Fargo's brows lifted as he glanced at Lisette. "I told the colonel you made me promise to see you to the border," she said.

"Ah, yes, so I did," Fargo said, and after a final handshake with the colonel he went outside to the Ovaro, feeling surprisingly strange without the scarlet jacket. Lisette followed him moments later and swung onto the brown gelding. "You know, I'm getting forgetful. That promise slipped my mind," Fargo remarked.

The tiny smile toyed with her lips. "I'm glad I remembered," she said.

"So am I," he said. "So am I." He rode beside her and saw that the top button of the deerskin vest had fallen open. Promises took all kinds of forms. It would be a slow trip back made of promises and pleasure and the kind of memories beyond forgetting. And another meaning to Mountie.

LOOKING FORWARD!
The following is the opening
section from the next novel in the exciting
Trailsman series from Signet:

THE TRAILSMAN #160
THE TORNADO TRAIL

Indian Territory, 1860,
In what will one day be Oklahoma,
A wild land scarred by trampling cattle,
Where Indian law is the only law . . .

The tall man sat on the pinto, gazing into the box canyon
below him. At the bottom of the narrow arroyo, a trickle
of water glinted silver, reflecting the midday sun. He
scanned the steep-cut banks and the dense thickets of
willow turning yellow in the warm spring air. High in
the tangled branches were clumps of dead leaves. Driftwood lay scattered on the banks. For a long moment he
let his eyes rest on the dark shape of the man lying facedown on the rocks. The only movement was the occasional flapping of wings from the half-dozen hawks
perched on the dead body. Skye Fargo's lake blue eyes
read what had happened there as easily as others read
words on a page. For a week he'd been searching for
Harvey Morgan. And now he'd found him.

With a sigh he chose a spot where the rocky wall gave
way to tumbled earth and headed the Ovaro down into

the ravine. The sure-footed pinto plunged down the crumbling bank, digging in its aft hooves and sliding partway down the slope. At the bottom, Fargo let the horse wander toward the tender green shoots by the babbling water.

He dismounted and walked slowly forward, striding over and around the jumbled driftwood and snarled branches. It had been some flash flood, he thought to himself as he stepped over a heavy log. This whole territory around north Texas was known for violent weather. Spring and summer were seasons when the big storms came, when white clouds would suddenly pile up and turn black while the wind whipped to a frenzy. If a man was lucky, there'd be only driving rain and ferocious lightning. But an unlucky man out in the open could get caught in a tornado, flash flood, or even have his head broken by lethal hailstones the size of eggs hurtling down from the sky.

Fargo clapped his hands loudly. The hawks flapped their dusty wings, retreating but reluctant to leave. From the distance of ten feet the stench of death assaulted him. He slipped his neckerchief up over his nose and moved forward. The carrion birds had picked the flesh from the back of the corpse, and in places the ribs and spine showed through the tattered strips of clothing. With the toe of his boot Fargo heaved the body over.

Harvey Morgan lay staring up at the sky, his face swollen, his eyes opaque and clouded white. His face and head were discolored, bruised, and battered, the top of his skull crushed. Fargo knelt down for a closer look. After a moment he stood and scoured the area. He found

Morgan's saddle, water-logged and wedged between two piles of driftwood. He hoisted it to his shoulder, noting the mark of the Circle M Ranch branded on either side, and carried it back toward the body.

What the hell had Harvey Morgan been doing down in a box canyon in the middle of a storm? Morgan had been ranching in north Texas for twenty years. If he'd got caught by bad hail, he'd have done what any man with a lick of experience would. First off, Morgan would have known it was useless to try to outride a storm. Instead he'd have dismounted, put his saddle over his head, and let his horse make a clean run for it. But it looked as though Morgan had also tried to take refuge in the canyon, where he'd been caught by a flash flood. That didn't make sense. Morgan knew this country like the back of his hand. He knew how the runoff water from a downpour could turn these ravines into raging rivers in a matter of minutes. Fargo was dead certain Harvey Morgan wouldn't be in the bottom of an arroyo in the middle of a storm. But it looked like that's what had happened. The incongruity pricked at his thoughts.

In any case, Morgan was dead. Fargo fetched a wool blanket from his saddlebag and rolled the body inside, securing it with rope. He tied the corpse on top of the pinto along with Morgan's saddle. Then he led the Ovaro out of the box canyon and across the wide, wind-swept grassland.

Harvey had been a fine man, generous and trustworthy, one of the most successful ranchers in all of north Texas. Fargo had known Morgan and his wife, Fiona, for many years. And now he had to break the news to Fiona

that her husband was dead. When Morgan had disappeared the week before and his horse had been found
without its saddle, she'd wired Fargo to come help in the
search. Well, he'd come and found Morgan, all right.
Finding him dead was bad enough, Fargo told himself.
But finding Harvey Morgan's skull crushed and his body
supposedly washed down the canyon by a flash flood
made Fargo uneasy, made him wonder if the rancher
might have been murdered.

The whole thing looked like a clever setup. But he
couldn't be sure of that. He decided not to share his suspicions with Fiona. Not at first. Not for a while yet.

"Get that Cayuse over here!" Fiona yelled to a cowhand as she pushed the chestnut hair out of her eyes and
donned her hat against the afternoon sun. The cowpoke
responded to her order, digging his spurs into the sides
of his mount while he dragged a lassoed calf toward the
fire and the waiting red-hot branding iron.

Fargo stood in a knot of onlookers, his foot hooked
over the bar of the corral fence, as he watched Fiona
Morgan direct the spring branding. He'd just ridden in
and found it in full swing. Fiona hadn't spotted him yet.

For the past month the ranchers of north Texas had
been preparing for the spring cattle drives. First, all the
hands from every ranch in the vicinity had been round-
ing up cattle, chasing them out of every coulee and gulch
for miles around where they'd wandered during the long
winter. Then the drovers had cut the giant herds, separating the longhorns by brands. An unbranded calf, called a
"slick," followed its branded mother, so the ranchers

knew which calves belonged to which ranch. And now the slick bull calves and heifers were about to get the mark of the Circle M Ranch burned into their hides. It was hot and hard work. And with Harvey Morgan gone, Fiona had taken on the job.

Fargo watched with admiration as she seized the red-hot iron and pressed it onto the flank of the calf that the cowhand had wrestled to the ground. She threw the weight of her slender and strong body against the iron to hold it steady. The calf struggled and brayed his protest as the smell of singed hair wafted on the fresh spring air. After a moment Fiona removed the sizzling brand and stood back. The cowpoke released the calf. It leaped to its feet and flew toward a cow that stood at a distance, pawing the ground nervously. The cowhands cheered.

"Okay," Fiona called out. "Get another slick over here before this fire's cooled down!"

She wiped the sweat from her brow, then spotted Fargo among the crowd. The smile left her face, and she removed her leather gloves, spoke briefly to the short black man kneeling beside the fire with bellows, and headed toward Fargo. As she drew near, he found himself once again marveling at her beauty. Her steady gray eyes showed a rare intelligence. The luster of her skin shone even through the streaks of dirt and sweat, while curling wisps of chestnut hair tumbled around her face and neck. The Levis and shirt she wore couldn't disguise the curves of her willowy body. She reached the fence and climbed over, landing gracefully on her feet beside Fargo.

"Follow me," he said.

Wordlessly she trailed behind as he led her away from the crowd around the corral and into the barn, where he'd left her husband's body. Fiona stopped short as her eyes adjusted to the dimness of the barn and she saw the blanketed form of the corpse lying on the hay beside the saddle. She stood for a long moment, and her eyes filled with tears.

"Where?" she asked, her voice choked.

"In a box canyon on the western border of your spread."

"How?"

"His skull's crushed and he's pretty battered," Fargo answered. He stopped a moment, but she hadn't flinched, so he went on. "His saddle was nearby. Looks like he got caught by a bad hailstorm and then a flash flood."

"What in hell was Harvey doing down in a canyon in a rainstorm?" Fiona asked, a touch of anger in her voice. She bit her lower lip as the tears rolled down her cheeks. She glanced at Fargo. "I don't believe that's what happened."

She was one smart woman, Fargo thought. Even in the midst of her grief, she had her wits about her. She had the same suspicions he had.

"Can you think of anybody who'd have wanted Harvey dead?" Fargo asked.

"Nobody," Fiona said. "Everybody liked Harvey." Her voice caught in her throat, and her knees weakened as she staggered a step. Fargo reached out and steadied her. At his touch she seemed to collapse, and he pulled her toward him as she dissolved into sobs. He held her close, his powerful arms around her warm curves, as she cried for a long time. Fargo kept his gaze fixed on the bundled form of Harvey Morgan. Finally she wiped her cheeks against her sleeve and backed away, avoiding his gaze.

"Thank you, Skye," she said. "Thank you for finding Harvey. You were always a good friend to him . . . to us. Come on to the house for dinner tonight, and I'll settle up with you. We'll bury him tomorrow morning."

"I'm sorry about Harvey," Fargo said. "And you don't need to pay me," he added.

Fiona didn't answer but turned and walked slowly out of the barn. Fargo watched as she stopped and spoke to two cowpokes hovering outside. Then she continued toward the big ranch house, walking as if in a daze.

The two ranch hands, a tall red-bearded fellow with a sunburned face and the short, wiry black man Fargo had seen stoking the fire came walking into the barn. They stopped when they spotted Fargo and the blanket bundle.

"Hell," the tall one said, pointing to Harvey's saddle on the floor. "Ole Harvey's done stopped his clock."

They both removed their hats. The short one's wiry hair had flecks of gray in it, and the bearded one was nearly bald. The two stood in silence for a moment, then turned to Fargo.

"You must be that fellow they call the Trailsman," the black man said. Fargo nodded assent. "We've heard tell a lot of tall tales about you. I'm Little John," he added, his white teeth flashing as he spoke. "And this here's Big

John." He jerked his thumb toward the carrot-topped giant.

"Miz Fiona said to go dig a spot for him out near that big cottonwood," Big John said. He shook his head sadly. "Don't know how this ranch is gonna run without Morgan around. Little John and I've been around here for a long time, but we ain't never seen things this bad before."

"How's that?" Fargo asked.

"There's a mortgage coming due," Little John put in. "And the bank's been putting the squeeze on Morgan. Last year he let most of the cowpokes go. Lot of hard feelings about that. And we're all working twice as hard. It ain't been easy. But if this ranch is going to be saved, Miz Morgan's going to have to sell every four-legged, two-horned critter on the spread."

"*If* we can get those longhorns up to market in time," Big John broke in. "This ranch is shorthanded already, but without Harvey . . . it's just going to get worse."

"We'd better get digging," Little John said, his brown eyes troubled. The two hands retrieved picks and shovels and left the barn. Fargo returned to the corral, his thoughts whirling. So, Harvey Morgan had fired a bunch of cowpokes the previous year. Maybe one of them had been mad enough to seek revenge. Or maybe one of the cowhands left was angry at how hard they all had to work with money tight. But angry enough to murder?

As Fargo neared the corral, a piece of paper nailed to a post and flapping in the wind drew his attention. It was a printed notice, some kind of handbill. He held it down flat and read:

REWARD: $500
FOR INFORMATION AND ASSISTANCE
IN RESCUING MY BELOVED DAUGHTER,
SUSANNAH,
CAPTURED TEN YEARS AGO BY THE CHOCTAW
TRIBE.
INQUIRIES: QUINCE PORTERFIELD, ESQ.
CARE OF PAULI'S BAR IN ELSVILLE.

Choctaws? Kidnapping a white girl? Fargo knew some Choctaws and spoke their language. The tribe lived up in the Indian Territory north of Texas. Choctaws were peaceable for the most part. Maybe they'd been riled up, and that's why they'd made off with the girl. Fargo reread the notice and wondered if she was still alive after ten years. That was a long time for a young white girl to be living with the Indians.

Fargo moved on toward the corral. Inside the fence, a greenhorn cowpoke vaulted toward a running calf, intending to tackle it, but landed nose down in the dust while the others laughed.

"Hey, I just heard Morgan's been found dead," a voice said quietly. Fargo glanced over and saw two gaunt cowpokes, both with the deep-lined faces and bowed legs that marked men who had spent years riding the range.

"No kidding."

"Yeah. Caught in a flash flood."

"Well, that's it for the Circle M. Take my word for

it—this ranch is going bust. Morgan's dead and that's the nail in the coffin."

"Hey, I heard Dick Denver's outfit's hiring. And he's paying good money—$30 a month."

"Yeah? Then let's get out of here before it goes belly up."

"I'm with ya."

Fargo watched as the two men sauntered away toward a low building that Fargo guessed was the bunkhouse. If the Circle M was mortgaged to the hilt and losing its cowboys, how was Fiona Morgan going to get the cattle to market? How was she going to get her herd hundreds of miles north to the buyers in Missouri or Kansas?

His mind full of questions, Fargo turned and watched as a very young and obviously green cowpoke wrestled a rambunctious heifer to the ground and another awkwardly applied the branding iron. At the touch of the fiery metal, the heifer bawled and jerked, blurring the brand. The two cowpokes swore as they let the calf up and it sped away. Fargo thought of Harvey Morgan. He'd been a good rancher, one of the most successful. And yet the Circle M was in dire straits. How the hell had that happened? Fargo wondered.

Fiona Morgan sat curled in a large chair by the unlit fireplace, her chestnut hair falling over one shoulder. The late afternoon sun spilled across the wide wooden planks in the great room of the ranch house.

"For the past five years the cattle just haven't been breeding," Fiona said, her gray eyes troubled. "At least, that's what Harvey thought. Usually a herd will double every three years, but ours hasn't." Her face was lined with worry and grief. "And we'd been doing so well for a while."

"Rustlers?" Fargo asked.

"We thought of that," Fiona said. "But none of the other ranchers were missing any cattle. Harvey even formed an association of locals, and they rode the lines for a year. But nobody caught any cattle thieves, so they gave up."

"Maybe the thieves were only after *your* cattle," Fargo said. "And too slick to get caught."

"Maybe," Fiona said thoughtfully. "Then last year one of our hands stole the payroll." Her voice turned bitter at the memory. "A kid named Blue Perkins."

"Blue Perkins," Fargo muttered. He knew that name from somewhere. He tried to remember where, but nothing came.

"Blue had worked at ranches around here before," Fiona said. "Came highly recommended by one of our neighbors. But he took two thousand dollars right out of Harvey's desk. We'd always trusted everybody who worked for us. Big John, Little John and Curly—why, they're just like family." Fiona blinked back the tears in her eyes. "Anyway, the Texas Rangers looked all over for Blue, but he just disappeared."

"A crooked cowpoke is an unusual animal," Fargo said. "Most of the boys I know are straight as arrows."

Fiona nodded assent.

"Right after that the Elsville bank came down hard on our mortgage," she continued. "The board of directors voted we'd have to pay now or lose the ranch. Oh, hell . . ."

Fiona bit her lip, and Fargo saw that she was barely holding her emotions in cheek.

"How much do you owe?" Fargo asked.

"Plenty," Fiona said. "Sixty thousand." She swallowed hard and her voice took on a defiant tone. "But I've got a good ten thousand head ready to go north. I can get eight bucks a head up there, and that would be plenty to pay off the debt and keep the ranch going. But I'm stuck for cash. The ranch hands are beginning to suspect I can't meet the payroll. And they're right, Fargo. Nobody's going to lend me any money. Not with the bank breathing down my neck on that mortgage."

Fargo heard a heavy tread across the veranda. Whoever it was had jinglebobs on his boots, whose sole purpose was to make a racket. If there was one thing Fargo hated, it was jinglebobs. Dandies and pompous asses wore them. That had been his experience.

Fiona jumped out of her chair to open the front door, and a tall, imposing man entered. Fargo was surprised to recognize Dick Denver. His hair had turned gray and his face had deeper line than it had when Fargo had met him years before down in El Paso. Denver's dark eyes still shone with the same keen intelligence, and expensive clothes hung on his wide shoulders. Dick Denver had been a big man in El Paso, a businessman, something to do with the mail service and the town bank. In fact, Dick Denver had practically run El Paso. So what the hell was he doing here? Dick Denver glanced toward Fargo but didn't seem to recognize him. He tipped his ivory hat to Fiona.

"Sorry to hear about Harvey," Dick said. "It's a real loss to all the ranchers around here."

"Thanks," Fiona replied. "Come on in. I'd like you to meet Skye Fargo." At the name, Dick Denver started and looked around, focusing on Fargo. A wide smile lit up his craggy face.

"Oh, the famous Mr. Fargo," Denver said, advancing toward him, hand outstretched. "I think we met once." Fargo rose and shook Denver's hand, remembering why he'd never liked the man. He was too smooth somehow. In El Paso, Fargo had had the feeling Denver had another game going on. But he hadn't stuck around long enough to find out if his intuitions were right.

"What are you doing in these parts?" Fargo asked.

Denver chuckled as though the answer to the question was evident.

"Why, I own the Double D," he said proudly. "Next spread over to the west. Four hundred square miles of the prettiest flatland in Texas and some of the biggest longhorns in the state."

"Dick's one of our best neighbors," Fiona put in. "He was a real help to us the year the blowflies got so bad and we ran out of axle grease and carbolic acid to treat the herd."

"I'm always glad to be of help to you," Dick said, ducking his head. "I'd like to talk to you about that very thing, Fiona," Dick said, glancing toward Fargo as if suggesting he leave the room.

"Skye's an old friend of ours—mine," Fiona said. "You can speak freely in front of him."

Denver cleared his throat and paced in front of the big stone fireplace for a moment or two. "Frankly, I know you're in trouble, Fiona," he said. "This afternoon six of your cowboys came riding over to my place to ask for a job. They said there's a rumor going around you can't meet payroll for the spring drive."

Fiona's face turned red, but she held her voice steady.

"So, the word's out," she said quietly.

"Yeah," Dick Denver said. "I know you're going through hard times. I just want to tell you my offer's still good."

Fiona looked away from him and clenched her hands.

"I'll—I'll have to think about that, Dick," she said.

"A pretty woman like you," Denver said, his voice low and silky smooth, "you ought to be living in town somewhere. You ought to—"

"Lay off her, Denver," Fargo cut in, his voice cold. He could see what was happening. He could see it all very clearly. Dick Denver, businessman that he was, saw an opportunity to get a good deal on a huge spread that would double his ranch. He'd come to put the squeeze on Fiona just when she was most vulnerable. At the sound of Fargo's voice, Dick Denver whirled about.

"This is between me and Miz Morgan," Denver spat. Then his voice softened. "Look, Fiona," he added, "I just want to be of help."

"Not right now," Fiona said. "I'll talk to you next week maybe."

Denver shook his head. "I've got to have your answer

tomorrow or never," he said. "My spring drive's ready to go up to Kansas City. If I buy you out, I'm taking both our herds up north. If not . . ." He paused and added darkly, "I'll do what I can at the Elsville Bank, Fiona. I'll use my influence. But the board of directors is really determined to call in your loan. One way or another, you're going to lose this ranch. Either I pay you for it. Or else the bank will just seize it. Your choice. I'm sorry. I'm just trying to help you out."

Dick Denver turned and strode across the floor, his boots jingling irritatingly. He let himself out without a backward glance. Fiona stood looking after him.

"Maybe he's right," she said thoughtfully. "Maybe I ought to just sell the ranch. Get out once and for all."

"What would Harvey do?" Fargo asked.

At the sound of his name, Fiona's face hardened, and a determined look came into her eyes. "What am I saying? I've got to be crazy! Harvey loved the Circle M. He put his whole life into building it up. I'll be damned if I'm going to let a little hard luck put me down."

"That sounds more like the Fiona Morgan I remember," Fargo said with a smile. For the first time all day, Fiona smiled too. Then her face darkened again.

"But if Dick Denver's heading up to Kansas City with his big herd, the prices will be low by the time I can straggle up there behind him," she said, thinking aloud. "If only there was a trail to the west of the Old Shawnee. A trail that went up to Wichita. The railroad's through there now, and I could get a good price in Wichita. But nobody's taken herds up through Choctaw country before."

"I'll help you, Fiona," Fargo said. She glanced at him gratefully.

"I—I didn't want to ask," she admitted. "Because I don't know how I'll pay you."

"We'll figure that out later," Fargo said. Fiona smiled again.

"Thank you, Skye." She sat thinking for a long moment. When she spoke again, her words were determined. "If I'm really going to get my cattle north, I need a thousand dollars to pay for supplies. And to hire the boys," she said. She pursed her lips. "It's no good, Skye. All I've got is two hundred."

"I've got three hundred I can put in," Fargo said. It was all he had on him, but Fargo figured he'd rather lay his money down on a long shot that they could keep Dick Denver from taking over the Circle M. It would be worth it.

"Thank you, Skye."

"That still leaves you short five," Fargo said. Suddenly he remembered the handbill tacked to the corral post. Quince Porterfield—that had been the name. He'd offered $500 to anyone who could get his daughter back from the Choctaws. They'd be going right through Choctaw territory. It was perfect. Quickly Fargo told Fiona his plan and she agreed. Ten minutes later, she was heading toward the corral to tell the ranch hands they'd be driving the cattle out at dawn. Meanwhile, Fargo was galloping off toward Elsville to find Quince Porterfield.

Pauli's Saloon was in full swing when Fargo arrived. The batwing doors swung outward as a man crashed into the street. Fargo stood back and then peered over the doors inside. A few dozen men were swinging fists and swinging chairs at one another. As he watched, a bottle of beer went flying through the air and smashed into the mirror over the bar. It shattered into a thousand silver pieces. The bartender, a portly man hunkered down behind the bar, scuttled away from the falling glass. Fargo slipped inside the saloon and grabbed the bartender as he passed.

"Hey, you!" Fargo shouted over the din. The bartender, expecting a fight, brought up his fists. "What's going on here?"

"Friday night!" the bartender shouted back as they ducked a flying chair.

"I'm looking for Quince Porterfield!"

"Real troublemaker!" The bartender pointed to a short red-faced man with ginger hair swinging his fists wildly in all directions and shouting. None of the other men, grappling nearby, took any notice of Porterfield. As Fargo watched, Porterfield stumbled, obviously drunk. Fargo stepped forward, shouldering his way through the roiling crowd.

A big black-haired man bumped against Fargo and whirled about, his eyes blazing. Fargo backed away, not eager for an unnecessary fistfight.

"You getting in my way, stranger?" the big man shouted. Without waiting for an answer, he swung a right, aiming at Fargo's jaw. But Fargo was too fast. He pulled back and the man's thick arm whistled through the air in a wide circle, throwing him off balance. He staggered a step at the same instant Fargo jammed a hard right into the man's belly. The breath left the man, and he gasped like a fish. Fargo followed with a powerful left that snapped the man's head upward. He sank to his knees and fell face forward onto the floor. Fargo looked around and spotted Quince Porterfield watching him intently. He took a step toward the old man, and Quince, thinking Fargo was coming for him, turned tail and fled toward the door. Fargo chased him out of the saloon and down the deserted street, dark with night, finally catching hold of Porterfield's arm.

"Hold on, there," Fargo said to the short man, who turned around, ready to fight. "I want to talk to you." Porterfield looked at him uncomprehendingly, his fists still in the air. "It's about your daughter."

Porterfield shook his head confusedly and lowered his fists.

"What do you want?" he said, his words slurred with booze.

"I hear you're offering a reward," Fargo said. "For your daughter."

"Indians got her," Porterfield muttered, shaking his head. "Goddamn redskin savages. Gotta get her back. Gotta kill those Indians."

"Look," Fargo said, breaking in. "At dawn there's a trail drive leaving from the Circle M. We're going right through Choctaw territory. You can come along, and I'll try to get your daughter back. I know those Indians and I can talk to them. We'll try to make a deal. But I want half the money up front. Pay the rest when we get her."

Quince Porterfield stood swaying in the middle of the

street, blinking his eyes and trying to focus on Fargo's face.

"Susannah," he said. "Got to get her back. Sure. Sure. Half the money up front. It's a deal." Porterfield stumbled a step forward and fell on his face in the middle of the street and lay there. Fargo swore and leaned down to seize the collar of the drunk old man. He pulled him down the street toward the town's one hotel.

The hotel desk clerk recognized Porterfield and seemed unsurprised to see the man unconscious. He directed Fargo to Room 2. Fargo propped Quince Porterfield against the wall while he threw his gear into the leather grip he found in the closet. After a few minutes, Porterfield roused himself enough to retrieve a wad of cash from beneath the mattress. They checked out of the hotel, collected Porterfield's stocky roan down at the livery, and headed out of Elsville.

The star-studded night sky glittered above them as they galloped on the trail northward toward the Circle M spread. Around them the dark, empty land seemed to stretch out forever. Fargo heard the yip of coyotes in the brush and the call of the burrowing owl. Once, as they were coming down a long slope, Fargo thought he heard hoofbeats on the trail behind them. He reined in and signaled Porterfield to do likewise, but he heard nothing behind them but the sounds of the night.

Fargo was relieved to discover that Quince Porterfield rode well even when he was drunk. Taking along a stranger on a cattle drive was always a risky proposition. The trail was rugged and it tested a man's character, not to mention his ability to stay in a saddle for fourteen hours a day.

Five miles from the Circle M, the trail descended into a steep ravine. The Ovaro took the slope gracefully, its powerful legs absorbing the impact of the fast descent. Fargo turned in the saddle and glanced back to see how Porterfield's roan handled the rough terrain.

Then he saw them. Above, on the rim of the arroyo and silhouetted against the stars, Fargo spotted several dark figures—men on horseback. An instant later he saw the blue glint of starlight on steel as the line of men silently raised their rifles.